THE BEST LAID PLANS

A SOCIALLY DISTANCED THORNTON VERMONT ROMANCE

CAMERON D. GARRIEPY

*This story is for everyone
whose best laid plans went awry this year.*

- Lust at first sight
- Slow burn
- Flirty texts
- Antici..............pation
- Neighbors to lovers
- Chickens
- An itty-bitty mistaken identity
- Semi-forced proximity
- Quaran-teammates
- 40ish LIs
- Sexy talk in a mountain swimming hole
- Masks and social distancing

THE BEST LAID PLANS

CHAPTER 1

Poppy Daley snapped her laptop shut with a huff. When she'd been assigned to moderate the department chair's remote-learning classes, she'd assumed it would be a simple task. Four weeks, they'd said at the faculty and staff meeting that closed Thornton College. Spring break to prepare, then two weeks of remote classes while the virus ran its course.

As Mother's Day approached, Professor Bixby still hadn't mastered the video conference software, and Poppy was still holed up at her parents' house taking virtual attendance and troubleshooting his connection issues from her father's desk.

It could have been worse. Her parents might have been holed up with her. Susie and Stewart Daley were weathering the global lockdown at a remote Scottish estate. In addition to the painting and hill climbing they'd planned for, her mother's sporadic messages suggested they were gardening and tending hens and shaggy cattle alongside the owners to feed the self-isolated artists' retreat.

Which left Poppy house sitting her childhood home in Catmint Gap instead of sheltering in place in her downtown Thornton apartment, tending the garden and hens they'd left behind. Indefinitely, if the governor and the college administration were to be believed.

Her email notification chimed, reminding her that Professor Bixby expected his lecture transcriptions at speeds that exceeded Poppy's abilities. The department's previous—and far more treasured—administrative assistant had retired at seventy-two, still typing eighty-five words per minute and requesting she be referred to as a secretary, regardless of the updated position title.

Poppy was more of an organizer-manager, less of a typist–and the department's weekly newsletter needed to be assembled, come to think of it. It would be a long afternoon.

She slid the slim computer across the kitchen table, reaching for her water. She could spare a few minutes for a walk out to the coop, check the nesting boxes for eggs, and pick some spinach for a salad on the way back.

Her parents kept a dozen hens in a large coop and run, screened from the house by a copse of her mother's legendary lilacs. Her mother spent more of Poppy's youth with her flowers than with her daughter. Poppy had once accused her mother of naming her after the wrong flower. Her mother pointed out that lilacs didn't talk back.

The chickens were oblivious to the pampered perennials as they pecked and scratched in the run.

Halfway back to the sunroom with her skirt pockets full of eggs and baby spinach leaves, a breeze picked up the lilacs' perfume.

She couldn't deny their beauty. The Daleys' three

acres, carved from wild mountain forest and meadow, were carefully planned to look wild and chaotic, with clusters of thriving, blossom-heavy lilacs arranged on the landscape. Tall, white Russian *Beauty of Moscows*, showy *Sensations*, Japanese tree lilacs with their lovely foliage. The heirloom *Ludwig Spaeths* with their late, extravagantly deep purple flowers. Potted *Tinkerbell* lilacs lined the walkway to the kitchen garden.

Poppy stopped among the mostly still sleeping allium beds. Pots and whiskey barrels waited for the herbs over-wintering in the greenhouse. The emerging garlic and leeks spiked optimistically up from the ground. The chives were rioting, flowering and spreading in their planter. She took a handful of tops, breathing their garlicky scent as they broke.

The crunch of tires on gravel announced an approaching car long before it appeared around the last turn of the long, private drive.

When Poppy was young, *Yankee Magazine* profiled her mother, publishing a photo essay of her lilac farm. The next spring people started arriving. Lilac tourists were few and far between, but it surprised her just how many people were willing to drive up a barely marked mountain road to ask someone they didn't know for a tour of their extravagant backyard. The numbers tapered over the years, but her mother still reported the odd flora tourist around Mother's Day.

The sound of tires on gravel meant strangers to Poppy's ears, no matter how many years passed.

Poppy tucked the chives into her pocket along with the spinach and went out to send the unexpected arrival packing. *Leave it to some spoiled traveler to assume that they would be welcome to view the lilacs despite the shelter-at-home orders.*

The car in front of the yellow *Primrose* lilac hedge had that buttery sound that only came from expensive engines. Taking in the windswept lines of the sporty hardtop, Poppy sighed in equal parts annoyance and vehicular lust.

The woman who stepped out of the car pushed back a honey and sable mane of hair with sunglasses that likely cost more than Poppy's entire work wardrobe.

"Nicky didn't mention there were lilacs… or a housekeeper."

"I'm sorry, but I'm going to have to ask…" Poppy began, then stopped as the woman's words sank in. "Excuse me?"

"I have a mask in my bag, but I can wait here. Please tell Nick that Elisha's here, and not to be surprised I'm a brunette."

Poppy resisted the urge to lob one of the eggs in her pocket at the interloper. The sack skirt with its big, deep pockets was one of her favorites, and it did have a bit of a vintage housedress vibe, but did she really look like the housekeeper?

"I'm sorry. Elisha, was it?" Poppy dusted her hands on the skirt. "There's no one called Nick on this mountain, as far as I know, and this is my house. I think you've taken a wrong turn. You're on Lilac Lane. And it's private."

The confident smile faltered, and Poppy pressed on, impatient to get back to making both lunch and some progress on Professor Bixby's notes, and just a *tiny* bit perturbed at being treated like the help by a woman so lovely she might have been synthetic.

"If you're looking for someone, I'd suggest taking a left at the bottom of the hill and heading towards Catmint Gap on Bobolink Road. Someone in the village should be able to help you."

Two points of color rose on the delicate cheekbones. "Forgive me. I'm familiar with the village. I teach at Thornton College. Of course you're right. I'm sure I took a wrong turn."

The ease with which the woman tipped her glasses back from her hair and covered her eyes without detriment to her silky blowout was downright unfair.

The taillights disappeared around a bend in the driveway before Poppy realized who the woman was. *I teach at the college... Elisha's here... surprised that I'm a brunette...*

She'd just run Professor Elisha McNair, darling of the Women's Studies department, off her parents' property.

CHAPTER 2

The network of trails winding through the forests of Catmint Gap, Vermont, hadn't been a selling point in January when Nick Cooper leased the "renovated mountain retreat" for six months. The photos of the cantilevered deck, soaring among the ice-glittered tree canopy, had sold him. After three failed network pitches and a Christmas spent dodging questions about his relationship status, he'd needed a break.

By the time the pandemic closed the economy, the trails provided a much needed break from his own brain. He would run through the woods with his empty backpack over his shoulders, following the blazes that led to Catmint Gap Road, then mask up and walk down the main route to the market. Freshly provisioned, Nick would unmask, run out Bobolink Road, over the bridge that crossed the ravine, turn right on Lilac Lane, then push hard up the last quarter mile once he reached the driveway to the cabin.

In March, the five mile loop left him winded and shaking. Now, with May's first real warmth soaking into the forest, he loped along, breathing deeply and noticing things.

Dawn, the cashier at the village market—a place which sold everything from milk, bread, and frozen peas, to candy and snacks, to cast iron pans, fishing lures, bait, and ammo, to gasoline and ice—said the couple who owned the property at the end of Lilac Lane were odd ducks, but nice enough. Last she'd heard, they were traveling in Europe, but got stuck there when the virus closed everything. Nick took that to mean they were unlikely to bother him up the mountain.

Lilac Lane. A fanciful, but appropriate name in its way. From the road marker just after the ravine it wound about a tenth of a mile up a gentle incline through young birch, oak, and maple forest to where it forked into the deep evergreen shade. In one direction, the secretive access road led him up to the cabin; in the other, two vast, wild lilac hedges framed his neighbor's entrance.

Before the birches and maples had leafed in, he'd been able to see down from the cabin's deck to the cleared acreage that must be the homestead, but the house remained hidden. Now, the entire property retreated beyond the rioting green and purple.

The sultry purr of an engine coupled with tires on damp, hard-packed dirt drew Nick out of his thoughts. He glanced up the road and saw Elisha's Jag crawling down the road.

Shit. She'd said she was coming up to drop off essentials. *Whatever that meant.*

He pulled his bandanna up over his mouth and nose and flagged her down. She stopped the car and the window glided down.

"Nicky!" The pet name should have sounded squeaky, but Elisha's voice was like everything else about her. Smooth, cultured, finely honed. Deeper than expected. They'd grown up together, leaving Nick immune to her charms and forgiving of her faults.

"I just met your neighbor. The Lilac Lady."

So much for Dawn's reliability. "I didn't think anyone was living there right now."

"I doubt you'll have any reason to run into her," Elisha said. "I have a box from Mimi and Grandpere for you in my trunk. Scotch from Grandpere, those Swiss cookies Mimi keeps in the pantry, and Grandpere sent books for you. Tell me how to find Joss's place, and I'll head up there and leave it for you while you finish your run."

Elisha spoke the cabin owner's name with warmth and ease. "Exactly how well do you know my landlord?"

"We were in the same class at Thornton College." She sighed. "That's all. I'm friendly with his wife."

But she's never been there, which means what exactly? His love of a good story never stopped, even if all he had to chew on right now was The Mystery of Elisha's Sex Life.

"Back up about fifty feet and turn around in the Lilac Lady's driveway. The fork is right there, but it's not marked. Kind of looks like a trailhead but it's the drive-way, I swear. You'll brush some laurel branches on the way through, then the road drops and curves before it rises up to the cabin. I'll be right behind you."

Nick waited until he saw the car disappear before

lowering his bandanna and jogging after her. The supplies in his backpack jostled, rubbing his shirt against his sweaty back.

He should have asked Elisha to drive the pack up the last quarter mile.

CHAPTER 3

"I know, I know," Poppy said to Mathilda, the plump Golden Laced Wyandotte hen who liked belly rubs and was occupying the picnic table near the run, "I'm wearing mascara. But it's because I like it, not because that woman thought I was the housekeeper."

Mathilda regarded her with aviary nonchalance before hopping down to scratch at an ants' nest she found in the grass.

The sun was out and the breeze was blowing fluffy clouds across the sky, so Poppy was free ranging with the chickens while she worked. The picnic table caught the last vestiges of the household internet connection, allowing Poppy to bring her laptop out and monitor Professor Bixby's classes.

The mascara was a whole lot of too little too late, but she did enjoy the effect. The thin veneer of professionalism she'd cultivated working for Thornton College's History Department had entirely faded since the lockdown started. She favored unstructured skirts with pockets and stretchy tees and tanks in her free time. Her freshly washed curls would look decidedly untamed after air drying without any product, but it didn't really matter. The chickens didn't care, her laptop's camera–like the mic--was off.

With the exception of snooty Elisha, Poppy hadn't seen anyone but the cashier at the Thornton Co-op in days.

Professor Bixby finished his video lecture, and Poppy watched as the individual tiles of his forty-two students closed. She emailed the attendance list, a summary of the lecture, and a transcript of the student questions from the chat to the professor's inbox. *If only he would learn to look at some of those things for himself...*

She was closing her computer when a lost Hemsworth wandered out of the woods.

Or, upon closer inspection, a previously undiscovered, Forty-Something Hemsworth? At least six rangy feet, soulful eyes and a generous mouth, with a twig in his hair, just where a few silver strands shot through the rich brown.

The laptop nearly slipped as Poppy shot to her feet, heart hammering.

"Oh, hey. Sorry," he said, coming to a stop as The Orpington Twins, Lavender and Buffy, flapped over to him. *Shameless hussies.* Forty-Something Hemsworth took in the ever-so-charming coop and run, the profusion of lilacs, even Poppy herself in a swift, unnerving gaze. "Did I stumble into some kind of fairy tale quest?"

Definitely not an actual Hemsworth...that accent was pure prep school with a touch of New York. Having spent her entire life in close proximity to a NESCAC college gave her an ear for it. Still criminally good looking.

Her pulse slowed. The Twins kept him at the edge of the clearing, conducting a thorough examination of his feet and ankles. If he was a criminal, their prey-animal instincts failed them. The two hens, sisters by choice, might have walked straight out of a Disney animation. Both broad and a little swaybacked with smooth feathers, one palest blue-gray, the other the color of a summer wheat field in an over-exposed Ridley Scott dream sequence, they circled the stranger's feet, clucking softly and picking at his shoelaces.

He'd better keep his distance; her masks were all in the house. How could she have anticipated company appearing from out of the woods in the form of a ridiculously attractive hiker?

"You're off the Horizon Trail, if that's where you were walking. This is private property."

He picked a dandelion and offered it to Lavender, who snatched the treat and hopped away, Buffy in her wake. "Lilac Lane?"

Poppy narrowed her eyes at him. Not a totally lost hiker, then.

"Nick Cooper." He started to offer his hand, then remembered and pushed it back into his pocket with an adorably awkward laugh. "I'm renting the Fullers' cabin for...well, for now."

Nicky didn't mention... So that was where Professor McNair was on her way to in that enviable car.

Poppy sighed. Of course *available, age-appropriate* Hemsworth lookalikes didn't wander into her parents' backyard. Mathilda flapped back onto the picnic table, greeting them both with the whirring chirp Poppy thought of as purring. "Poppy Daley. My mother cultivates the lilacs."

Nick grinned, charmed by Mathilda. "And you keep the hens?"

Stung, Poppy snatched up her laptop. "Yes. I keep the hens." She gestured to a nearby hemlock stand. "You can pick up the Horizon Trail about 40 yards that way."

Mustering the small dignity afforded to her by Maybelline Lash Sensational, Poppy spun on her heel and made for the barn, hoping Nick Cooper didn't notice the chicken poop on her flip-flop heel.

CHAPTER 4

"Y ou owe me," Nick said into the phone. "You didn't tell me she was pretty. And not retired. I swallowed not only my foot, but my ankle and most of my shin."

Elisha laughed. "I mistook her for your housekeeper. What makes you think I'm going to be any help?"

"You let me think my retired neighbors were down there, not a woman my age who's probably their daughter."

"I didn't know." She laughed again, musical and unrepentant. "And what can you do? This whole lockdown scenario is less than ideal for romantic gestures."

"Whoa." Nick pulled the phone away from his face for a second, as though Elisha could see his expression. "Who said *romantic*?"

"You called me asking what you could do for your pretty, not-retired neighbor…"

Elisha was often right. Infuriatingly so. She also often had the answers. Infuriatingly.

"Did you make it into the pastry shop in town before all this?" Nick imagined her hand waving in the direction of the window of her airy loft, one of three upscale condos carved out of a barn on a hillside north of the college. *All this...* The unobstructed view of the valley priceless. Nick wondered if her self-quarantine was made easier by the gilded sunsets she watched every night.

She would worry about her grandparents. She would worry about Ben. But he didn't mention them. "I didn't. Probably should have, huh?"

"Call them and order the lilac woman some chocolate croissants. The owner is delivering orders until she can reopen."

"Let me guess," Nick said. "You two got pedicures together before the salons closed?"

"No. Frankly, she drives me crazy, but her chocolate croissants are a decent alternative to sex."

Nick wasn't sure anything made of flour and butter was quite that good. "Why does the Princess of Pomfret even have a list of alternatives to sex?"

"I hate that nickname." She paused for a long moment. "And I'm not interested in sex right now. Too many complications. Croissants, however, can be forgiven by sufficient running and lifting."

Nick heard her unspoken closing of the topic. "So, I should order a chocolate croissant delivery from that bakery to say I'm sorry to my neighbor." *My very pretty, very much not-retired-matron neighbor who makes keeping chickens very appealing.*

"I'll text you the link. If your lilac girl's the irresponsible type, she'll turn up at your door in sexy lingerie to say thank you."

"She's not my lilac girl—"

But Elisha ended the call. Nick peered out over the forest canopy in the direction of Lilac Lane, unable to unsee the image of Poppy Daley, all those nearly blue-black curls tumbling over soft shoulders, smoldering up at him from beneath long, sooty lashes.

Fantasy Poppy wasn't wearing scraps of satin and lace. Nick found everyday underthings far sexier than delicate, complicated straps and netting. Easier to slide hands under, easier to discard en route to sweet curves and warm flesh.

When Elisha's text disturbed his runaway imagination, Nick clicked the link and called the bakery straightaway. Whether she thanked him or not, he owed Poppy an apology, and he was too practical to leave an imaginary girl outside in the woods in her underwear. She'd get eaten alive.

If it was his fantasy, that was his privilege.

CHAPTER 5

*P*oppy replayed Nick Cooper's arrival in the yard all the following morning, when she should have been working on Professor Dancy's proposal to hire additional distance TA's should the fall semester be impacted. In each replay, she regained a piece of her lost dignity, until finally she was about to dismiss him with the icy cool of a modern Grace Kelly…when her phone rang. She answered, despite not recognizing the number, but only because her parents were helpless with technology and an ocean away.

Her self-redemption vision popped like a soap bubble.

"Hi, Poppy, it's Kate Pease. I'm in your driveway with a delivery."

"You're what?" She gathered her manners. The owner of her favorite pastry shop wasn't to blame for her distraction. "Hi Kate. I didn't order anything, though…"

"You have an admirer. Andy and Danielle are manning the phones from their apartment, so I don't know who they are, but I like their style."

"I'd love to say hi, but..." Poppy didn't finish her sentence.

Thank god I don't have to face her right now. Kate had been several years ahead of her in school; she came home from Paris about the time Poppy graduated from Thornton Union, but they'd gotten to know one another supplying department meetings with coffee and pastries in Poppy's early days at her new job. Poppy suspected no one had ever confused outspoken, chic Kate Pease with a housekeeper... or referred to her as the keeper of hens.

"Social distancing. Understood. I'll leave the box on the front porch," Kate said. "How are you doing up here all alone...where are your folks, anyway?"

Poppy was rescued by the doorbell-chime notification of a Zoom lecture starting. "Scotland. I'm doing okay, Kate, but I have to go... work...The door's unlocked. Do you mind sticking the box inside where it's cool?"

"Perfect. Take care, Poppy." Kate ended the call before Poppy could apologize for her haste, so Poppy clicked to open Professor Bixby's classroom notes. She turned over a blank notebook page and adjusted her reading glasses. The front door opened and closed.

She rewarded herself for staying awake through a lecture on the dynastic complications of pre-William of Orange England speculating about the sender of the mystery pastries in the foyer.

The telltale hot pink box contained a half-dozen chocolate croissants. The note read, *A thousand apologies to the Lady of the Lilacs. I've heard some things about these pastries—your neighbor N. -PS, my foot tasted terrible.*

Poppy felt a blush rise right up from her belly and

wash over her cheeks. Lady of the Lilacs was so much nicer than Hen Keeper, but what did he mean about hearing things?

The foot bit made her laugh.

So much for Grace Kelly; she liked Nick's style, too.

CHAPTER 6

$\mathcal{O}$n Sunday morning, Nick took his laptop out to the deck, hoping the robin's egg sky would settle his brain enough to pound out the pages Sanjay asked for. His erstwhile partner in crime was pitching a sci-fi for one of the streaming networks, and while Nick didn't want to ride his friend's coattails too much, Sanjay still had connections.

Nick had a nuclear meltdown, a string of rejections, and no good ideas.

That Sanjay was asking at all was something to be grateful for, which left a bad taste in Nick's mouth, but again. Gratitude.

Poppy Daley hadn't turned up at his door, lingerie or otherwise, but it was the twenty-first century and there *was* a pandemic on. People didn't just drop by.

He didn't know what he would do if she did. It wasn't like he could invite her in, ply her with booze and conversation, and convince her to fool around—enticing though that thought was.

Regardless, he hoped she enjoyed the treats, especially those supposedly-better-than-sex croissants…

And there it was, that little *whoosh* in his gut that was faster than the words in his brain, faster than his fingers on the keys. *The croissants. A snippet of conversation.* He was typing before he really knew where he planned to go with it, using the bare bones Sanjay had given him to frame out a scene. Once upon a time, his dialogue was a hot commodity. Sex, pastries and charming a beautiful woman wasn't revolutionary, but it was a start, and it made space travel instantly relatable.

Three hours later, he emailed his pages to Sanjay and brought the laptop inside. He'd missed the dopamine hit of a good writing session. His blood fizzed; ideas raced in circles in his brain. *Christ, he was humming.* The trouble was, sheltering at home on a mountain a half hour from a civilization on hold left him with none of his former outlets.

He'd run, then. Take the Horizon Trail past the Daley's property again. If he were lucky, Poppy would be out with the chickens, and he could get a second chance, this time with the power of croissants by his side.

His libido was on overdrive along with all his other systems. One idle thought of the woman down the mountain, and he was thinking of the way she'd lick the flakes of pastry from her fingertips, how her lashes would flutter down and she'd sigh, maybe let out a little moan of pleasure…

Stop it, Nick. You can't go running like this. It's indecent. 'Hello, random passersby, please excuse this erection. I was thinking about watching a woman eat.'

Better to focus on what had bothered her and how to

really make it right. Because for a moment, she'd been wary but not unkind, flushed with sunshine and surprise, and he'd liked her. With the exception of his family, he'd been alone on this mountain for a long time, and it would be nice to have a friend.

Maybe more than a friend on the other side of the lockdown, if that ship hadn't sailed.

The blood rushed out of his groin. He'd more or less made her sound like a farmhand; decidedly unsmooth. But that wasn't all of it. He knew female appreciation, and he'd seen it in her eyes for a moment. Bending over to tie his shoes, he considered that.

He didn't flatter himself she knew who he was. Even if she was into obscure TV writing trivia, it wasn't like television writers had faces... His *name* had snuffed out the appreciation even before he'd verbally stung her.

He walked into the woods, stopping to stretch every few yards until he picked up the blazes for the trail. Heading down the mountain, picking up a rhythm, he pondered his social networks, wondering if they knew someone in common. His little meltdown was more or less public knowledge... It was possible they knew someone in common from school...

"Fuck." The problem was right here in Vermont. *I mistook her for your housekeeper.*

Elisha was a prickly thing. Whipsmart, beautiful, privileged. She elevated benign self-involvement to an artform. Snobbish to a fault until she let you in. And she'd been to the house on Lilac Lane. What had she said to Poppy?

More importantly, how had Elisha established herself —accidentally or otherwise—in relation to *him*?

CHAPTER 7

*P*oppy slept in on Sunday, waking in time to assemble a Caprese salad for one and the fixings for a pitcher of Paloma cocktails before her Zoom brunch date at noon. Before brunch could be savored, however, her mother's voice reminding her to wash the sheets had to be banished, so Poppy gathered the sheets from all three beds, even the ones she wasn't using, and hauled them down to the laundry room.

As far as Poppy, Meg, and Nisha were concerned, three single, professional women in their late-middle-thirties were almost obligated to mark the seventh morning of the week with breakfast cocktails and outrageous food. The lockdown measures had separated the three friends, but if their weekly tradition could survive ten years, it could outlast a social distance directive.

So, a homemade meal at her parents' kitchen table wasn't exactly her favorite Irish breakfast at Temple in Thornton, or the *huevos rancheros* from that fabulous little Mexican place in Vergennes, but her friends' faces on her laptop screen beat Professor Bixby and his students any day of the week.

Catmint Gap didn't boast much in the way of provisions, or people: four hundred souls, a general store that was also a gas station and the post office, a seasonal creemee stand, and Singing Bowl Ski Area on the back side of the gap. But a short drive south along Gooseneck Creek, in neighboring Blueberry Hill, was a hidden gem of a year-round farmer's market.

The owner had thrown open the doors–literally–despite the occasional May morning with a lingering chill, to keep her patrons and vendors safe. Poppy's early morning trip yielded fresh bread, hothouse tomatoes and basil, some fresh cow's milk mozzarella, and a little much-needed human interaction.

By quarter of noon, she only needed to pop the bread —and the last of the chocolate croissants from Sweet Pease, courtesy of flutter-inducing, sadly-involved-with-Professor-McNair Nick—in the toaster, but first she needed to get the clean sheets on the line to dry before the showers moved in later in the afternoon.

Ignoring the chickens *bawks* and squeaks for treats, Poppy snapped out the sheets and pinned them to the clothesline that ran between the chicken coop and a sturdy ash tree at the back of the yard, then took herself inside to pour a pint-glass-sized Paloma and fire up the laptop.

CHAPTER 8

*I*t didn't take Nick long to reach the hemlock grove beyond Poppy's place. He decided to think about the fact that it was already "Poppy's place" in his head later. The lilacs were already fading, but the scent lingered where the woods gave way to the Daleys' yard.

The hens were in their run, which to his eye looked nicer than most screened-in porches. His landlord was a builder, and a fine one if the renovations to the cabin were any indicator. He wondered if Joss Fuller had built the chickens' palatial quarters, which looked like a miniature version of the Small New England Colonial With Rooms Added house that occupied the heart of the property.

Feminine laughter rang out from the direction of the house. He'd assumed she was alone like him, but maybe not. Maybe she had sisters. Or a girlfriend. Maybe she had a *quaranteam*. He'd never been a loner until this winter, and while he was bearing isolation relatively well, it wasn't for everyone.

Between him and a glimpse of answers were three full sets of butter yellow sheets dancing in the breeze. The breeze which kicked up, turning over the silver backs of the ash leaves over his head. He peered west through the trees and noticed an ominous gray-green cast to the sky.

He pulled out his phone and prayed to gods of cell signals for enough data to check the satellite forecast. While it was loading, the first drops of rain began to fall.

His mother's housekeeper hadn't taught him how to fold a fitted sheet for nothing. *Thank you, Mariela. I've been training for this since I was eleven.*

He gathered the pillowcases one by one, folding and stacking them in the Shaker laundry basket left out with the washing. The flat sheets were easy, if a little unwieldy. Finally, only the fitted sheets remained.

Three times he recited Mariela's fitted-sheets instructions to himself, completing the complex folds in increasingly better time and execution.

Nick shuddered to think what Poppy would think if she appeared while he was up to his actual elbows in her bed linens.

Don't think about Poppy and bed...

By the time he tucked the last sheet in the basket, the summer shower was falling in earnest.

Nick scooped up the basket and looked around. An open shed near the coop for chicken keeping tools and supplies offered enough shelter to keep the basket dry. Nick left it inside, perched on a latched metal cabinet. He headed back to the Horizon trail with the smell of sun-dried cotton and warm rain on his hands, and a hot-as-hell vision in his imagination of Poppy Daley tumbled in those sheets wearing nothing but her shiny dark curls.

CHAPTER 9

*P*oppy was halfway through a third Paloma, heavy on the tequila—Nisha was halfway through *way* too much information about her new sexting relationship—when she realized it was pouring.

"Shit, the sheets!"

Poppy dashed up from the kitchen table, calling back over her shoulder, "I'll be right back!"

Nisha and Meg's laughter followed her outside. She dodged the rain, keeping under the older trees with larger canopies as she made her way to the forest's edge where the chicken coop and clothesline marked the end of civilization

Where she stopped short because her sheets were…gone.

"What the fuck?" Poppy giggled at her own outburst. Her mother hated swearing, and Poppy'd had just enough alcohol to feel gloriously rebellious. Especially as her mother was thousands of miles and who knew how long from being home.

Fat drops of warm rain plopped on her shoulders as Poppy searched the yard, the trees, and the chicken coop in vain, a weird sinking feeling building in her belly. Her mother loved those stupid sheets. *Only line dry them, Poppy. The dryer is terrible for the cotton...*

Her shirt was soaked and her buzz was fading fast. She ducked under the chicken shed roof to get herself together, and there it was, the Shaker laundry basket. Inside, rather impressively folded, were the missing sheets.

She glanced at the woods, wondering what kind of perv snuck off a hiking trail to fold someone's laundry and move it out of the rain. While it wasn't unheard of for strangers to appear via the driveway, the only person to appear in the backyard was Nick Cooper. Having stumbled upon her once by accident, he was unlikely to repeat the mistake. And while she questioned his taste in women, he didn't strike her as a total weirdo. Or a bedsheet fetishist.

Except...

There, by the clothespin bucket painted to look like a ladybug. A damp clump of mud in the crosshatch of a hiking shoe sole, and crushed in it, a purple striped piece of foliage. Ignoring the rain once more, Poppy made her way to the clue, skipping a little when she confirmed her hunch.

"Ha!" She leaned over to free the leaf from the mud. Waxy, indigo and maroon. A hosta leaf, and such rare-colored hostas grew in abundance just one large parcel of land up the hill, in the shade around the Fullers' cabin.

In which Nick Cooper now resided.

Her belly flopped over. He'd visited? Intentionally?

And folded her sheets to save them from the rain? And disappeared into the forest again like some kind of laundry guardian angel who also sent decadent apology baskets and dated expensive, brilliant women?

Meg and Nisha would have a field day…

Meg and Nisha!

Poppy dashed to the lean-to, grabbed the laundry, and raced back to the house, hoping her friends were still online. It was time to confess what a weird week she was having.

Her friends were useless. They giggled about the interference of masks when attempting to jump the bones of the hottie up the hill. The existence of Professor McNair didn't faze them at all.

In the end, Poppy decided the neighborly thing—the polite thing—to do, was to thank him with a gift of her own.

While the rain wore itself out, Poppy made up a gift basket, thanking the hens and her mother's well-stocked gifting drawer as she worked. She put on some music while she assembled trays of oatmeal butterscotch cookies and packed a dozen eggs. The lilacs had browned, but there were Siberian iris and mint along the driveway. She cut a small bouquet, wrapped it in a damp kitchen towel, and tucked the flowers in a glass milk bottle.

What else would a guy like Nick need or want?

Who even was a guy like Nick?

While the cookies were in the oven, she Googled "Nick Cooper." There had to be a million of them. She tried "Nick Cooper Elisha McNair," and under the Images tab found a photo of the two of them at a charity party in

Newport five years before. The caption described him as "TV writer N. Cooper."

The resulting narrowed results were all recent and none friendly. It seemed Nick had gone up against some powerful executives over a cancelled show. He'd given a scathing interview, accusing network leadership of sexism, racism, nepotism…in detail and by name.

And been blacklisted.

It took some reading, but four dozen cooled cookies later, Poppy had an idea of who Nick was and just why he was holed up in the Fullers' cabin.

She wrapped half the cookies in another kitchen towel, suddenly paralyzed with worry, wondering if cookies, eggs, and flowers constituted the lamest thanks ever given. She dug around in the liquor cabinet for a bottle of something unopened, coming up with a bottle of Coppers Gin. Her father did love the drink-local movement..

Buck up, Daley. You're only being friendly. It's not like you're planning to get him drunk and take advantage. You can't get closer than six feet anyway. And he has a girlfriend whose car is worth more than your annual salary.

She tied her hair back and laced up her sneakers. The Horizon trail was the long way around. She'd just take the driveway like a regular person.

As she walked, she mulled over her internet research. True, Elisha's name had led her to the right Nick, but other than a society page snapshot from half a decade ago, there were no other obvious links between them. *Were they simply discrete, too boring to be on the internet, were they not really an item?*

Her questions–hopes?–gave way to nerves as she

rounded the last curve of driveway and the cabin came into view. Unlike her parents' flowery fairytale glade, the clearing around the Fullers' cabin was wilder, despite the profusion of shade perennials and whimsical outdoor furniture. Even the surrounding forest seemed deeper, cooler, and more secretive.

Mustering what little dignity she retained where Nick Cooper was concerned, Poppy marched up to the front door and knocked.

*N*ick was enjoying an excellent shower fantasy involving Poppy and that warm, soft rainstorm when the brisk knocking on the cabin door interrupted.

"Jesus, Elisha. Call first," he muttered. He turned the water cold for a second to douse the daydream situation, then killed the spray. He grabbed his Columbia Prep flannels from the hook on the bathroom door and toweled his wet, too-long hair on the way to the door.

"Look, it's great that your grandfa–" Nick flung open the door expecting some variation on Elisha's fair, statuesque good looks. "Poppy?"

She was waiting at the bottom of the steps, a reasonable distance from the front door. The filtered sunlight lent her an underwater quality in the verdant air.

Down boy. She was all curves and curls and freckles and...luscious. Snug tee, skirt with pockets. Utterly practical. He wouldn't change a thing. Even the fine sheen of sweat on her upper lip from trekking up the hill was inviting.

More so was the open approval in her eyes as they traveled over his naked torso. Christ, he was still wet from the shower. He hadn't even dried off. If he didn't slow his roll, she'd know exactly what he'd been up to.

She licked her lips and looked down at the picnic basket she was carrying. Like Red Riding Hood at the Wolf's door. He'd like to devour her. *Damned pandemic...*

Reality was more effective than the cold water.

"Hey. I walked up to say thanks for saving my laundry from the rain." She set the basket on the top of the steps and backed down again. "It was sweet of you. And the bakery delivery. You didn't need to do that."

He peered into the basket. Booze? Eggs? Cookies? *Jackpot.* "I definitely did. I can still taste my foot after that hen comment."

Her lips turned up and laughter lit her eyes. "I can forgive almost anything after Kate Pease's chocolate croissants. You chose wisely. But I have to ask, what have you heard about them?"

A tiny wrinkle appeared between her brows when she was uncertain. Nick wanted to smooth it away with a kiss. There was no ignoring Elisha's comparisons between flaky pastries and sex now. Or visions of melting chocolate and Poppy Daley's lips. The celibate life had suited him just fine until he met this woman.

"A friend of mine says they're better than sex." He cleared his throat when his voice caught like an embarrassed teenager.

"Oh." She pressed her lips together to bite back a laugh and shrugged lightly. "That's fair."

No, it really wasn't. I could do better than a French baked good if given the opportunity.

"Anyway," Poppy continued, "you fold fitted sheets like a pro, and you saved me having to rewash them. They'd have gotten splattered in the rain..." Poppy trailed off, looking away. A blush rose up the tantalizing vee of skin revealed by her top. "So I'm returning the gift basket favor."

Nick got the sense she was gearing up to depart. Now that she was here, he didn't want her to leave. He couldn't invite her in, but he could keep her chatting. "How did you know it was me?"

Her shoulders straightened a little. She flicked a glance at the mounds of dark red and blue foliage that surrounded the property. "You left a hosta leaf behind in a clod of dirt. Nan Fuller is known for these hostas. I put it together."

"And here I was thinking I was so subtle." He pulled the door closed behind him and sat on the arm of an Adirondack chair on the porch. "Was it creepy? I'm sorry if it was."

One corner of Poppy's smile lifted, revealing a wry dimple that begged to be kissed. "A little? But useful-creepy, not icky-creepy."

"Useful-creepy..." *Oh, he liked her.* He leaned over, rummaging in the basket. "Would you like some..." He pulled out the bottle. "Gin?"

"It's a work night."

He shrugged, playing it cool and tucking the bottle back in the basket. "At least help me eat the cookies?"

"You don't want to save some for Professor McNair?"

"Elisha?" *Is that what she thought?* He pulled a cookie

from the cloth she'd wrapped them in, taking a bite while his friend's name waited between them. "Why would I save some for her?"

Poppy's confusion played out on her face for a beat. "You're not… I thought you two were… oh."

CHAPTER 11

*H*e just sat there, eating his cookie and looking like some kind of Ivy League Men of the Woods calendar page, stray droplets from the shower still clinging to his collarbone, and *oh, dear lord, Poppy, do not look at his chest hair!*

Too late. Water clung there, too, and he'd obviously pulled those flannel pants on over wet legs. Poppy had no idea what to do with her hands. Or her eyes. And then ever-so-casually he lets it drop that he's not involved with Thornton College's Second Sexiest Professor.

"Seriously, have a cookie. If I eat all of these, I'll have to run into the Gap every day, which means I'll buy more supplies and need to wash my masks more often. It's a whole hassle."

He was teasing her. It was like someone had flipped a switch and they were old friends. He nudged the picnic basket toward her with his foot. His feet were narrow, with long toes and high arches. Poppy had never given a moment's thought about a foot's attractiveness, but Nick's were just as well-formed as the rest of him seemed to be.

She stretched up the stairs to grab a cookie, leaning on the railing at the bottom step to maintain distance once she had it. "I wouldn't want you to risk unnecessary exposure; or put Dawn at risk." She bit into the cookie and threw caution to the wind. *Would it really hurt to flirt?* There was nowhere it could go. She looked up at him through her lashes. "Who knows where you've been?"

"So true." He nodded gravely, the twinkle in his eyes spoiling the gravitas. "Out-of-work television writers are notorious flouters of CDC guidelines."

She might have missed the flicker of vulnerability that moved across his features, had she not violated his privacy all over the internet only hours before. And of course, she was used to putting on a brave face. Disappointing her mother since the beginning of time, disappointing any number of lovers over the years, disappointing herself as the years crept by and she settled for her perfectly acceptable, stable little life in her lovely, safe, boring hometown while the wide world adventured on without her.

"I've never really been anywhere. My parents travel now, but when I was younger my mom was all about her lilacs...and my dad worked. We rented a house in Maine for a week a couple of summers..." She trailed off, embarrassed at the confession.

"This place is gorgeous, and if my *friend* is to be believed, not completely bereft of culture, despite being several hours from New York City." Nick shifted into the seat of the chair, his expression gentle and direct. "I can think of worse places to be."

A lump rose in Poppy's throat; she covered it with a final bite of her cookie before attempting to regain the playful mood. "Maybe when all this is done, I'll run off to Paris or marry a New Zealander like they do in romcoms."

"Have a fling with an inappropriate neighbor, that sort of thing?" He raised one brow in a smolder that loosed a thousand butterflies in Poppy's belly.

"Exactly." She heard the squeak in her voice, the rush of air from her lungs. He was out of her league in just about every way. Poppy pushed herself to standing. "My dad calls home on Sundays. Like actually-the-landline-calls-home. I should get going. Thank you again, for the sheets, and the snacks."

"Poppy, wait." Nick stood, too, coming to the top of the porch stairs. His hair had begun to dry, curling slightly at the tips. "Can I get your number?"

"My what? You– Why?" She snapped her mouth shut. *Get it together, Daley.*

He grinned. "That way I can text you before the next time I turn up in your backyard."

CHAPTER 12

*W*hen Nick first started writing for television, he worked on a medical drama for a second tier cable network. In its third season, he penned the soliloquy that changed the direction of his career.

The character, a middle-aged orderly named Horatio, professed his love to one of the nurses at the end of a harrowing night shift. Sadie, the nurse Horatio loved, wasn't the most beautiful actress in the cast, or the bravest character…but she had a good heart. The orderly saw what was lovely in Sadie, and dug deep to find a way to tell her so.

Nick tapped into his own most vulnerable veins for that dialogue, and as a result millions of viewers across the nation fell in love with his work. Not one of them knew the name Nick Cooper, but it was true just the same.

Nick leveraged his success. He moved to better shows, better contracts with better networks. He met Sanjay, and within a few years their partnership wrote its own checks, but the truth was, he hadn't written anything quite as eloquent as Horatio's declaration since.

The look of confusion in Poppy's eyes when he asked for her phone number made him want to dig deep again. To call her ten minutes later as she was walking through her front door with the perfect words to tell her just how lovely she was, compelling, sexy, and above all…*likable*.

Of course, Murphy's Law dictated that if you *wanted* to call a woman immediately after you got her phone number, the universe prevented you from having a free moment for the next forty-eight hours. Nick had been living in the Fullers' cabin for weeks with nothing to do but contemplate his navel. Suddenly real life got interesting, and he was fielding work emails and furiously drafting the only real writing he'd done all year.

Sanjay, in his infinite wisdom, forwarded Sunday morning's pages directly to their agent. Nick wasn't sure, without expensive lunches, expensive cocktails, or expensive rounds of golf, how anything in entertainment got done, but by the end of the day, Margot had a premium cable network considering a bid against the streaming service. Nick knew, given his recent history, there was no time to mess around.

He sent his share of a pilot script to Sanjay after two furious days with too little sleep, too little food, and too many thoughts of Poppy fueled by her excellent butterscotch oatmeal cookies.

Feeling that he'd earned himself a drink, Nick pulled the bottle of gin from Poppy's gift basket. He poured himself a double and wandered out to the deck to consider his future.

The gin was smooth and bright, with an orangey note that surprised him. On an empty stomach, it didn't take much to go to his head.

A crushed-velvet twilight was settling over the Green Mountains; the Bluetooth speaker he kept near while he was working played a melody that slipped under his skin. So much more than a stretch of National Forest stood between him and his neighbor.

And yet, he pulled out his phone.

Hey pretty Poppy

When the telltale rolling ellipsis appeared, his pulse skipped. A single question mark appeared on the screen.

?

It's Nick

He could learn to love those little indicator bubbles.

Hi neighbor

The gin was excellent. Poppy was intoxicating. Nick took a seat in one of the lounge chairs on the deck and topped off his drink. He was going to seduce his neighbor the old fashioned way.

With text.

CHAPTER 13

Pretty Poppy? She felt about thirty years too old to be charmed by that, and yet. She'd known it was Nick even as she sent the ? for confirmation.

It was a soft evening. Humid, but cooling. The light was falling fast, and the last of the hens were making their way into the coop for the night. Poppy checked the enclosure for any eggs she might have overlooked while keeping an eye on her phone.

She hadn't really expected to hear from him, certain he was only being nice to make up for the gaffe the day they met. Sure he was only being neighborly. They were more or less alone on the hillside. There weren't many other homesteaders on Bobolink Road once you left the village of Catmint Gap—which itself was about six hundred souls.

How was your chat with your dad?

He remembered. *Swoon.* She nudged Lavender and Buffy up the ramp while typing her reply.

Good. What do you know about Munro Bagging?

Sounds filthy, let's do it

She hoped the very slight breeze didn't carry her unladylike snort up the hill to where he was.

It's hiking. In Scotland.
My dad is doing it. There are 281 specific peaks you climb
Anyway, he bagged the tallest one last week. He was proud of himself

I'll Google that. How've you been? It's been ages

It's been two days

It felt like ages, though. Was it possible to miss someone you'd only just met? She wished for excuses to see him, had indulged in more than a few conversations with Mathilda in which she'd posed the question, "What if Nick *were* interested?"

Golden Laced Wyandottes weren't known for their relationship advice.

Two days too long. Had a sudden onset case of work

She rolled her eyes. *How nice to not have Professor Eustace Bixby the Luddite looking to you for everything.*

How sad for you

> It is sad. I meant to call you straight away and
> convince you to do something with me.
> Something appropriately six feet apart, of course 😉

The wink at the end made her laugh, even as desire fluttered in her chest and burst over her skin.

> We can't bag a Munro in Vermont, but we could take
> the Horizon Trail to Arcadia Falls? Tomorrow's
> supposed to be warm enough for swimming

Oh God, was he asking her on a date? Dating was touch and go *before* the global pandemic.

Poppy wasn't sure she was ready for a five mile round trip hike with masks, or for that matter wearing a bathing suit in front of Nick Cooper. On the other hand, she didn't want to lose this chance. Best to play to her strengths.

> Not sure I'm ready for hiking in a mask. Some of us aren't
> regular trail runners
> We could have lunch? Meet at my picnic table at one
> tomorrow afternoon?

At some point while she'd loitered in the yard texting with Nick, the sun had slipped behind the trees, headed for the hidden horizon. A lone firefly winked from the edge of the yard. Poppy could relate, waiting in the near-dark for a reply.

Her phone pinged, and she saluted in the direction of the little light. "Good luck."

Your picnic table sounds perfect. What can I bring?

She sighed happily. *Just your Forty-Something Hemsworth self.*

Surprise me

Hopefully I'll do a better job than last time

Poppy puzzled over that for a moment before clarity dawned. He was teasing her. The last time he'd surprised her at her picnic table was the day they met.

He really hadn't done a very good job that day, but she liked his chances for tomorrow.

Before bed, she brewed iced tea and baked cornbread. Before work, she picked baby spinach and kale, chives, and violets for salads with poached eggs.

Poppy raided her mother's hoard of table linens and pottery, setting places for their lunch at opposite corners of the picnic table. A sunny yellow tablecloth, two blue striped placemats. The country pottery dinnerware from Provence and chunky glassware from a local flea market.

All through Professor Bixby's morning lecture and discussion sections, Poppy reviewed a series of protocols for the fall. She was increasingly uncertain about the summer and fall semesters on campus, but the administration was still trying to work out how to handle the confusion of information. Underneath all of that, awareness of Nick's arrival hummed like a train down distant tracks. Something inevitable—thrilling and dangerous—headed her way.

She'd tried not to fuss over her appearance, but a little Lash Sensational and some curl serum to tame her mane never hurt. And she might have picked a casual dress with a particularly flattering neckline.

Maybe.

She arranged lunch on a covered serving tray (it was going to be a shock, when her parents finally got home, to move back to her singleton apartment in Thornton with her singleton dishes and lack of formal serving pieces), and carried everything outside at quarter to one, only to find Nick already there, crouched by the chicken run, apparently deep in conversation with the hens.

"…what you girls like best, and it's yours. Just get me in with the lady of the house. What is it? Worms? Exotic insects? I'll fly them in from wherever."

A happy shiver rolled down Poppy's back as she paused there to drink in the sight of him. He *did* like her. And he was flirting with the flock to get to her. Or at least playing at it. Stagecoach Mary, Belle Star, CJ, and Mathilda were all perched on the old wooden ladder in the run, clucking and chirping at him.

"She's right behind me? With lunch? And I should share?" Nick looked back over his shoulder, winked at her, and turned back to his audience. "Play it cool, ladies. I'll be back. With snacks."

Poppy inhaled through her nose and rebooted her brain. He was impossibly handsome, unfolding from his crouch in the dappled sun. He'd dressed up. Of course, today's polo shirt and khaki shorts were practically formalwear after Sunday evening's damp flannel pajama bottoms.

She should have requested the damp pajama bottoms.

"Can I help? I have a mask." He plucked at a pale gray bandanna he wore at his throat, pulling it up over his nose. "I decided it's time to update the highwayman concept."

Poppy wiggled her hips. "Mine's in my pocket, but we're all set. Table for two, distance style. You're over there." She tilted her chin at the far seat.

She set out the food and laughed as they danced around serving themselves while avoiding close proximity. When plates were filled and seats were taken, she found herself suddenly shy.

"Tell me what you do for work," Nick said, buttering half a wedge of cornbread.

Poppy wondered if he was clairvoyant. "I'm an administrative assistant in the history department at Thornton College. These days I run interference for a professor who's... technologically challenged. I actually live in town, but my parents asked me to stay here while they were in Scotland for a month, and then the pandemic hit, and they got stuck there, and..." She shook her head. "That's not what you asked."

"I would have." He tucked into his salad. "How did you make poached eggs and green things taste this good?"

She rolled her eyes. "The green things were growing until this morning, and the eggs are courtesy of your new BFFs over there. It's all in the sourcing." She took a moment to dredge a cornbread crust through a pool of runny yolk and olive oil. "And I'm an excellent cook."

"Well, that's sexy as hell." Nick was running a finger

absentmindedly along the top of his tea glass. "Seriously. I mean, that you can cook, and that you own it."

"Thanks." She didn't know what else to say; she wanted that absentminded finger tracing circles on her body.

"Truly," he said, catching her gaze. "My writing partner and I got into some hot water—I write for TV, I probably should have said—over a fight with the network that started with a showrunner." Poppy watched as the easy humor flashed into something else. Passion? Fury, even. "This douchebag—pardon my French—didn't think the protag on this prime-time romcom we were pitching would go for a heroine who owned her talents. It was twenty-fucking-nineteen, and this guy's all, 'Nobody watches a show where some smartass woman gets laughs for being better at stuff than the guy.'" Nick stabbed at his kale, then waved his fork to bring home his next point. "The best part was, *that wasn't even the humor of the show.* It was smarter than that, but this mouth breather got his panties in a wad—" He set his fork down with a chuckle Poppy could only describe as rueful, and echoed her earlier sentiment. "But that's not what you asked."

"I would have," she said softly. "What happened?"

"He pulled the equivalent of telling his dad on me. I ended up on the other side of a very expensive desk at the network. I switched off every filter I've ever developed. I unleashed my considerable—and colorful—vocabulary on a bigger fish who held my reputation in his sweaty little hands. And once I'd laid out in devastating detail exactly what I thought of every banal, misogynistic, cliched piece of horse manure his network was responsible for, he blacklisted me. My partner started out in the UK. He rode out the storm on connections I didn't have, and I owe him. That's what I was doing the last few days. Paying up."

Their lunches lay untouched between them. Poppy was stunned. She hadn't expected him to be so honest. Her covert Googling felt dirty.

"I Googled you."

His laughter burst out of him. It was big, deep laughter, the kind that had to run its course. The hens scattered in the run. "Of course you did. Do I live up to my front page hits?"

"You're not angry?"

"I'm not angry." His laughter dried up, replaced by heat, banked and playful in his eyes. "God help me, Poppy, I wish I could kiss you right now."

Being rendered speechless was a figure of speech. Poppy had been certain of that until Nick spoke those words. Every nerve in her body thrilled. Awareness pooled between her thighs. Intelligent discourse dried up on her tongue.

"I must be losing my touch. This is the part where I hoped you'd at least say…" He bridged his fingers under his chin and fluttered his lashes like Bugs Bunny in the old cartoons her dad loved. "'Gosh, Nick. Me, too. Damned pandemic.'"

Poppy's brain glitched again and heat rushed to her cheeks. He was infuriating. And wonderful. She wanted to play, too. Even if it terrified her.

She met his eyes and spoke slowly, deliberately. "Gosh, Nick. Me, too. Damned pandemic."

By the end of the sentence, her voice had gone husky, and she wasn't sure they were still talking about kissing.

The picnic table didn't seem like a safe enough distance anymore.

Nick broke the moment with a deep drag of air. Poppy was glad to see she wasn't the only one who needed steadying.

"I brought dessert," he said. "And two blankets. And a bag of black oil sunflower seeds. The woman at the garden center said chickens love them."

ick spread out the two Navajo blankets he'd brought, keeping an imaginary Sanjay between them for distance and as an imaginary chaperone. With a little flourish to hide the aching lust rampaging through him, he set out slices of Sweet Pease's dark chocolate torte in protective compostable boxes. Curbside pick-up champion, him.

He went back for the bag of sunflower seeds. "Can the chickens come out?"

Poppy narrowed her eyes in the direction of the chickens' run. "After the cake. Or you won't get any."

She knelt, setting her tea glass next to her cake. Nick wanted to ask if she had more dresses like that. Enough to wear every day for the rest of her life. It was deceptively simple, wrapping around her waist like an embrace, revealing an intriguing shadow between her breasts, flaring over those hips she'd shimmied when she'd mentioned her mask. And it held what Nick knew to be the most treasured of aspects in a dress: pockets.

She had pale legs with rounded calves and slim ankles. Her shoulders and arms were more deeply tanned, liberally dusted with freckles. Not a regular sunbather, then, but she spent time outside.

She caught him staring. "Nick?"

"Poppy?"

"You surprised me."

He still wanted to kiss her. If he was being honest, he wanted a lot more than to kiss her. The chemistry between them was palpable. He hadn't felt this kind of instant pull in a long time, if ever. In another time, in different circumstances, he wondered if they'd have tangled already.

"I'm glad." He watched her taste the cake, torturing himself imagining the feel of her mouth, the taste of chocolate and woman. His own dessert paled in comparison.

"What if we quarantined together?" It was a crazy idea when they barely knew one another, but it felt right. "Not together, together, but...Lock down in our places on the mountain for two weeks to be safe, get to know each other...responsibly...then see if all this flirt adds up."

"Can we do that?"

Nick watched her emotions play out across her expression like cloud shadows on a sun-drenched field: curiosity, uncertainty, desire, doubt. Humor won out, and her smile gave him hope.

"This feels like the role playing exercises we used to have to do in high school sex ed."

Nick leaned back on his blanket. Every time he thought he had her figured out, she lobbed a curveball. "Consent works for me. So does disclosure. I'll go first. I saw Elisha that day she rolled up to your house like the anomaly she is. We kept our distance outside. She and I go back to Kindergarten, for the record. We grew up together. No hanky-panky. Ever. I mask up when I'm in town or the village. Which I've done twice since we met. No symptoms except some hay fever stuff when the pollen is high."

Poppy sat up, primly tucking the hem of her dress around her knees and holding up a hand to tick items off on her fingers. "Professor McNair, in my driveway. Mrs. Thompson at the Co-op in Thornton for some groceries last week, masked. The farmers' market in Blueberry Hill on Sunday, masked and outdoors. And Mrs. Halladay at 1693 Bobolink. Through her kitchen window. I water her garden and leave her some eggs once a week–there's a rotation going on the Catmint Gap Facebook page." She dropped her hand and looked at him. "It could work."

Three words, as effective as a caress.

CHAPTER 15

Poppy woke on Thursday to a world distinctly out of sync with the sunshine and birdsong in her heart.

Relentless rain battered the house, leaving the air clammy and the house dark. Professor Bixby didn't have any classes, but there were always unfinished department projects to work on. Poppy brewed a pot of coffee and opened her computer. If she logged her hours early in the day, she could start writing out a list for Coulson's Garden Center. Her mother had emailed drawings for the raised vegetable garden beds and requested that Poppy use their credit card to make the necessary purchases. She also wanted Poppy to put the plants in the ground. It wasn't really her wheelhouse, but Poppy hadn't really thought living on the mountain full time with the chickens was going to be her wheelhouse either.

At least she wouldn't have to wander the aisles of plants. She could order it all online and drive her dad's old Volvo into town. The folks at Coulson's would load it up and send her on her way. Fewer interactions meant no delays in the fourteen days between now and Nick.

He'd stayed for hours the night before, long after the mosquitoes came out. They'd wrapped up in the Navajo blankets and talked about the lilacs and growing up in Catmint Gap. She told him about Meg and Nisha and their brunch tradition. He showed her photos of his parents sharing a hammock at their new house in Connecticut, and lamented that he hadn't adopted a dog before the pandemic. She'd Googled Ben Nevis to explain Munroe Bagging, but he was determined to misunderstand it in the name of dirty jokes.

She'd had to lend him a flashlight to walk back to his cabin. It felt like summer camp.

A text popped up on her phone.

Couldn't sleep. Made you something

When the Spotify playlist opened with a vintage power ballad, Poppy had to laugh. Guns N' Roses was a little before her time, but she appreciated the sentiment.

My to-do listed needed a soundtrack x

She sent the kiss without thinking, but it was too late to take it back. His reply was swift.

I"ll keep track of those for later

Her face felt hot. She wanted to fill the screen with little x's for him to tally up for later, even while she wanted to take it back and diffuse his laser-focused flirting.

Soundtracks? To-do lists?

> Kisses, gorgeous. One of these nights, you should tell me what kind of kisses you like best. I'll practice.

Poppy swallowed. Her fingers were actually trembling as she attempted to play it cool.

Practice on what, up there all on your own?

The typing indicators bubbled away for a moment before his answer arrived.

> I worked on a sitcom for a while. Google "French kissing cupcake"
> Come to think of it… Let's have cupcakes at the end of our quarantine. And French kissing

How was she going to make it two weeks? He was tormenting her. She was about to Google his suggestion, when another text popped up.

> You're Googling it now, aren't you? That's hot

She laughed out loud.

Stop it

> Can't help it. You're adorable

Gotta go. FaceTime with Sanjay. FaceTime with you later?

Nick Cooper might still be a bit of a mystery, but she'd give him this much: when he had an idea, he committed to it.

CHAPTER 16

Poppy hadn't said no to FaceTime, but Nick figured as long as it was outdoors and from a safe distance, actual face time was far preferable. He still had her flashlight, and a good neighbor should return things they borrow.

He set out around five, figuring Poppy would be done with her work hours by then, flashlight in one hand, paper grocery bag in the other. In it, he'd stashed Laurent Marchand's Scotch and Marianne's cookies.

Any chance I can get that face time now?

The rain had let up, but the sky was still dark and the trees overhead were shaking off the accumulated drops. Poppy didn't reply straight away, but Nick held out hope she was home and not busy. Her company had quickly become the highlight of his day.

On the way down his driveway, Nick applied to the neighborhood Facebook page. He'd never been a joiner, but he was living off Bobolink Road now, and being around Poppy made him want to belong. It turned out the Mrs. Halladay Poppy mentioned had a whole host of helpers, bringing in her newspaper and her milk—*people still had milk delivered here?*—watering her garden, taking the trash cans to the street and back. Nick signed himself up for garden duty and made a mental note to mask up and stop by to introduce himself before taking a specific shift.

Nick took his time walking down the last curve of his driveway and turned up Poppy's, enjoying the landscaping, hoping for a reply to save him from leaving the flashlight and heading home to be alone with his whiskey and cookies.

Hi. Yeah. I just got in from getting the eggs

Can I tempt you back outside?

?

knock knock

Her face appeared, peeking around the front door. Her hair was pulled up, spilling out of a messy bun piled high on her head. "When you said you were going to text first, I assumed I'd have enough time to change out of pajama pants."

"You've seen mine," he said. A guy could only hope she was also dripping wet from a shower and topless, but he doubted she routinely did her chores half-nude.

Down boy.

"What's in the bag?"

Nick shifted the bag to both hands and held it up. "You'll have to come out here to find out."

She pursed her lips, considering some unknown options. Nick decided he could watch her face for hours. "Come around the house. There's a screen room in the back."

He found the screen room on the shady side of the house, out of sight of the coop and picnic table. Poppy sat cross-legged on a wicker chaise; to Nick, she appeared poised for flight. She wore a soft-looking, gray ribbed tank and a pair of cotton lounge pants patterned with vintage-looking pairs of cherries.

He held out her flashlight.

"You can just leave that wherever," she said. She twisted her fingers together in her lap and avoided looking directly at him.

"Is it a bad time?" He should have asked her before coming down here. His manners were slipping. "I can go. No harm, no foul."

"No." Poppy dropped her hands. "It's just...I don't have anything... I didn't plan food or..."

He sat lightly on the nearest surface, a wicker lawn interpretation of a loveseat, and set down the paper bag. "I didn't come here for you to cater to me. I just wanted to see you. In fact, I brought Scotch and cookies. A traditional Cooper family—" He counted backward on his fingers. "Third visit gift."

She tilted her head. "Scotch?"

Nick reached into the bag for his offerings. "And cookies. I got the Scotch from a family friend—Elisha's grandfather is a collector. He sent me a bottle he wasn't going to keep or drink, but thought I'd like—and his wife always has these in the house." He set them on a nearby table. "That's what Elisha was doing up here the other day. Playing delivery girl."

Poppy snorted. "Sorry, that was mean. It's just, Professor McNair is hardly anyone's delivery girl."

"I'm glad she was ours. Cookie?" He opened the box of Matterhorn cookies and slid it across the table in her direction.

"I never say no to—" Poppy gingerly picked up the box and plucked a cookie from the package. "Butter biscuits with fine Swiss chocolate and honey nougat slivers. Okay, these sound lovely." She glanced warily at the bottle of Auchentoshan twelve year single malt. "Should I grab some glasses?"

"I promise. It won't bite. And if you don't like it, it'll just last longer up at the cabin."

By the third pour, doled out lingeringly over the sleeve of Matterhorns, a jar of olives and a frozen pizza Poppy found in the chest freezer in the garage, they'd delved into the dangerous territory of movies, books, and music.

An intimate, sleepy softness stole over the porch as darkness fell. Poppy was curled into the corner of her chaise, cradling her glass of whiskey.

"I'd probably get kicked out of the department if they knew I mostly read Regency romances."

"Shirtless dukes and heaving bosoms and all that?" Nick sat forward, leaning his elbows on his knees. "Sexy."

"Well, yeah," she said. "But I love the clothes and the carriages and stuff. It's so far away from here."

"I'm mostly in it for the stolen kisses in alcoves, lingering gloved caresses, that kind of thing."

Her gaze snapped up. "Don't tease."

"I dated a romance writer for a while a few years ago. Let's just say, she had a required reading list." When Poppy's eyes widened, he smiled. "I developed a certain appreciation for the genre, though I still prefer a good political thriller when I'm not researching."

"No thanks," she said, wrinkling her nose and sipping from her glass. A wicked twinkle appeared in her eyes. "So, what have you read?"

"Full confession." Nick leaned back, taking his drink with him. "I am bad with author names and titles, but there were two in a series with Scandal in it, and one definitely not Regency one that was darker."

The mischief in her expression heated and intensified. Her gaze traveled over him, settling on his mouth. Nick felt it like a physical touch. "Medieval? Tudor?"

"Victorian," he said. The air thickened under her scrutiny. She was full of surprises. Shy one moment, assured the next. Finding her comfort zones was quickly becoming his favorite pastime. "So buttoned up on the outside."

"I think I know the ones you mean. Definitely…" she paused. "A *little* more graphic."

"A little?" And here he was thinking he was an insider. "Tell me more, Ms. Daley, about your shocking reading habits."

CHAPTER 17

"**I** guess I don't hate Scotch."

Calamity Jane and Stagecoach Mary were sitting on the woodpile, complacently picking bugs from the firewood while Poppy sifted the sand in the run. The rest of the girls were puttering around under the long-faded forsythia.

"I hope you're all in the mood for watermelon this afternoon, because I have a date this evening." To punctuate the statement, she emptied the sifter—a contraption her mother had rigged from a pitchfork and some metal hardware cloth—into the wheelbarrow. "And I need to shower, because I have no intention of smelling like chicken shit, even at a responsible six feet."

Belle Star and Donna burst out from under the shrubs, Donna squawking, Belle making a guttural groaning noise. Belle had a worm, and was determined to swallow her prize before Donna could steal it, but the fracas was bringing the rest of the flock to attention.

Poppy laughed as Belle led everyone but Jane and Mary on a merry chase.

"You two have something figured out, don't you?"

She wheeled the chicken poop to the compost pile, a task at odds with her rosy thoughts. Nick had stayed until nearly midnight. They'd covered his unabashed love of both David Bowie and power ballads, and Poppy's admission that she was pretty much happy listening to whatever was on the radio unless the lyrics were cruel or made her sad.

Poppy always listened to the lyrics.

She'd told him about her first kiss—in a barn on a school field trip to a living history site in the seventh grade. Danny Hill had tried to stick his tongue too far down her throat and she'd gagged.

"I will do my level best to manage more finesse when the time comes," Nick said, holding her gaze until she had to look away, only to find herself staring at his lips.

He'd confessed to intentionally skipping an entire day's scheduled tours during his educational trip to Italy in high school to go to the beach with some Danish girls they met at a nightclub they shouldn't have been at the night before.

She tipped the wheelbarrow with a laugh. He was pretty far removed from Italy now. Wiping her forehead with the hem of her shirt, she considered that truth. In so many ways, he was unlike any guy she'd ever met. The feelings he'd woken had slept so long she'd stopped waiting to feel them again.

She'd settled. Falling for Nick wouldn't be settling, but it would be dangerous.

"Come watch the sunset tomorrow from the cabin's

deck," he'd said. "Actually, that's not right. You can't see the sun much at all…come see the changing sky with me."

He'd promised wine and snacks. Then tied her up in knots of wanting.

"I think about making out with you out there all the time. Sunset. Sunrise. Noon. It's a gorgeous view, and since I'd really, really like to monopolize your attention in future, I think it's only fair to invite you to see it properly at least once."

The very blunt way he spoke of his desire, his funny, flirtatious texts—this was the kind of seduction Poppy had always dreamed of, though she'd never put it in words. He was the kind of man she'd always fantasized about. Smart, witty, kind, playful, and he was extraordinarily easy on the eyes.

There's always a catch.

Isn't there?

When Poppy returned, Calamity Jane and Belle Star had returned to the flock. The hens were making their way toward the garden beds, which were still covered in their winter mulch and staked down. Poppy stowed the wheelbarrow and lured the chickens back to their run with a sheet pan of watermelon slices.

She left her skepticism in the run with the birds, determined to enjoy her evening soaring among the evergreens with Nick Cooper.

$\mathcal{N}$ick liked Nan Fuller.

They were of an age, and Nick suspected she was the kind of girl he would have overlooked in school and later regretted not knowing. He'd spent two nights at the Fullers' inn in the valley west of Thornton proper before moving up to Catmint Gap, and was thoroughly charmed by the whole family.

Between the inn, Joss's contracting business, their kids, and being connected in some way, it seemed, to the entire hamlet, they barely had time to breathe, let alone check in on the grown-ass man renting their cabin. Frankly, Nick found them to be refreshingly low-maintenance hosts, even pre-pandemic.

When Nan called several days later, out of the blue, he was instantly suspicious.

"Elisha says you've been exploring the neighborhood on the Horizon Trail."

"It's a great workout. And you can't beat the views." His wayward thoughts strayed to Poppy in her dress, eating chocolate torte and devastating him with her inexpert flirting.

"Joss and I were just thinking, if you're into trails, you should consider the Faye's Hollow loop. It's an old trail; the trailhead isn't marked. It's only a few miles and not difficult. There are maps on the shelf in the sleeping loft. There's a swimming hole—Faye's Hollow—halfway around." Nan paused, and Nick would have sworn she knew exactly what was afoot on Lilac Lane. "And we never run into anyone out there."

He *definitely* liked Nan Fuller.

Nick had paid attention to Poppy's clues as the days passed, to the warp and weft of her work and chores. Hew knew she didn't have classes to monitor that day, but remembered she'd been to town to pick up plants for her parents' garden a few days past.

Hey Gorgeous, what's up?

While he waited for a reply, Nick opened the SignUp-Genius page for Loretta Halladay's garden watering team.

Typing up departmental Zoom mtg notes. You?

Trying to get a date with a beautiful woman. Do you like my chances?

I don't know. You're a tough sell. What's she like?

Mid 80s, limited mobility, keeps a lot of guys on a string from the looks of it

He chuckled at the little bubbles, imagining Poppy's blushes and laughter, wondering which combination he'd earned. Wishing he could see it for himself.

Watch out. She'll eat you for breakfast, young man

Definitely rock the highwayman-style bandanna-mask look for Loretta Halladay...

Srsly, tho. That's sweet of you. The chickens approve

Do they? You know I crave their approval

Is that it? I thought you were using them to get into my knickers?

Sweet mother of undergarments, she was going to kill him dead.

Say knickers again, and my poor imagination will just explode. God, Poppy

Who knew? Sry 😊

On a less volatile note, can I help you with the garden later? I am excellent at following instruction

That sounds promising
I'm done with work at 2. Do you have work gloves?

Had he called her flirting inexpert?

CHAPTER 19

*N*ick *was* excellent at following instruction. He dug holes for tomato plants and moved planters and trellises according to her mother's drawings; he hauled bags of fertilizer and coiled hoses, all without breaking their six-foot treaty.

He got wet, filthy, and sweaty. In short, scrumptious. Poppy developed a new appreciation for male forearms.

He asked questions and absorbed information about the garden at an alarming pace. Poppy could almost see the information organizing itself in his brain for later use.

She'd never known a writer before. Not personally. The way he soaked in trivia and filed away knowledge about everything fascinated her. She wondered if, some-day, when *all this flirt* was over and Nick was restored to his career, she and her parents' lilac-and-hen-riddled retreat would appear in some television show.

The idea bloomed like a melancholy flower behind her sternum. There was no dislodging it, so she carried on working across the garden from him, listening to his stories of writers' room shenanigans, episodes that never aired, and pitches that never made it out of executive offices.

It was near-dark when they laid down the last of the thick layer of salt marsh hay mulch.

"Where do you get this stuff up here?" Nick breathed in a handful of the sweet, matted hay. "I remember the smell. The Marchands—Elisha's grandparents—their gardener swore by it, but they live near the ocean."

"My mother pays someone to drive a truckload up from Newburyport at the end of every summer. She keeps it in the hayloft. I tossed down a couple of bales this morning after I raked out the chicken run." Poppy broke apart a bale and tucked some hay around a pair of heirloom Black Krim tomato seedlings. "Of course her family has a gardener and lives by the sea."

She snuck a glance at Nick, feeling bad for snarking about his childhood friend, but he didn't appear offended. He just spread the last of his hay bale in the squash beds.

"She and I lived in the same building, " he said. "Doorman who slipped us Starbursts. Cleaning lady. My dad was an investment account manager for NexBank until he retired last year. He was careful and smart with his own portfolio. We had money. My sister and I had great educations, tutors, we played instruments and did sports. Ski vacations, trips to Jamaica, Disney World, and Europe, all that stuff. Elisha's mother's family owns a huge chunk of Jamestown, Rhode Island, as well as a vineyard in France, and the McNairs are one of those families whose money is kind of nameless and sourceless. They're just..*rich*. People like my folks find them aspirational. Basically, they're like aliens who walk among us."

It was hard to hate her when Nick described her like that.

"How about a beer?" Poppy said, leaning against the shed wall and swiping the sweat from her hairline.

"Perfect." Nick sat on the picnic table.

Poppy stopped a moment to recall the look of him there, the fireflies coming out behind him as the last of the peachy daylight melted away, before she went back to the house. She returned with two bottles of local beer. She wasn't a huge beer drinker, but a summer wheat brew went down cool and fresh on the heels of a long afternoon with her hands in the soil.

"Play hooky with me tomorrow," Nick said, picking his bottle up from where she left it on the table.

"Is it hooky if I don't have to work?"

"Come out and play with me tomorrow." He picked at the bottle label. "Have you heard of Faye's Hollow?"

"I haven't been there since my dad used to take me when I was a kid." She'd loved the hike through the woods and the pristine scoop of rock that formed the swimming hole. Not a pond, but a granite basin between spillways fed by springs higher up on the mountain. More rare in her mountains than in the neighboring White Mountains of New Hampshire. The trail was old, marked by rock cairns instead of painted blazes. "How did you find it?"

"I didn't. Nan Fuller suggested it. She heard from a blonde bird in a Jaguar that I liked trail running." He traced a drop of condensation down the glass neck. "And the view in this neck of the woods."

"It's one of my favorite places," she said, mesmerized by his finger and the water drop, "you'll love it." Never in her life had a guy tried so hard to impress her. He was ruining her for the slim pickings left back in Thornton, and yet that little blossom of sadness vined its way into her thoughts. A little drop of poison in the sweet wine of their flirtation. "Most of the trail is actually a cart road from the early eighteen-hundreds. It's wide enough to walk together and keep some distance. No masks needed unless we meet other people along the way. When are we going?"

"This heat isn't going anywhere. How about you text me when you're ready to go in the morning?" Nick drank deeply from his bottle. "June missed the memo that deep summer isn't until next month."

"Summer in Vermont is a fickle beast," Poppy said. "And that sounds like a plan." Her beer was empty, and their plans were made, but she wasn't sure she could let him go just yet. "The mosquitoes will find us in about a minute and a half. If you don't have other plans, stay for another drink on the porch. You can tell me about growing up in the city."

CHAPTER 20

When ten the next morning rolled around, Poppy met Nick at the small, lichen-covered cairn at the bottom of Lilac Lane in a red and white polka dot halter swim top, surf shorts, and hiking sandals. With her ink-dark curls held back in a bandanna, she looked like Gidget set loose in an REI outlet.

Damned pandemic.

"Good morning. I brought you a coffee... if you want it." He shifted his backpack to one shoulder, pulled a travel mug from one side pocket, and gave her an over-the-top smolder. "Any chance of you for breakfast?"

Her lashes fluttered down briefly and she pulled her bottom lip under her front teeth. When she opened her eyes and reached for the mug, he saw answering heat there, but something else that gave him pause. He'd crossed a line there, but he wasn't sure which one.

"Hey, sorry. Didn't mean to be predatory before coffee."

Poppy's eyes went wide. "Oh, no. I mean…That wasn't? I—"

And just as quickly as the desire, tenderness shot through him. He wanted to take her hand and follow her into the woods, let her take him down this trail and show him her history. He wanted to cradle her against his body and watch the sky all morning until they lost track of where they ended and the universe began.

How the hell had it happened so fast?

Poppy started to walk, the sway of her hips in the surf shorts his true north as he fell into step on the far side of the long under-used cart road. "Faye's Hollow is named for the region's most famous ghost, you know."

"Tell me."

She didn't say anything right away, only took a deep breath and gazed up into the trees.

The sun pierced the canopy in bars, but the early June air was thick with unseasonable humidity. Not five minutes into the walk, and sweat was beading on Nick's hairline, but the green-gold of the forest shone through Poppy's stray curls like a halo and she had a ghost story to tell him. Life was good.

"Nick?"

"Yeah?"

"If I say something, will you promise to take it at face value and not assume I'm being manipulative or anything?"

He stopped, wishing he could touch her. Wishing he could somehow physically convey that she could trust him, though they didn't know one another well in the traditional sense. "I promise."

She stopped, too. "What you said before, when I

was…not upset. I wasn't." She blushed a little but spoke directly into his eyes. "I have never in my life wanted more to be on the breakfast menu, but I know that you're not here forever, and it's in my best interests to remind myself of that. You just caught me being a little sad about it." She took a deep breath and smiled. "But that's on me, and I don't want it to change what's between us for now."

She was courageous. He hadn't even had the guts to consider that, never mind put words to it, for all his ability with them.

"Nothing's changed, Poppy." In truth, everything was changing, and he was surprisingly okay with it, but he went for the flirt to reassure her. "And we're halfway to *breakfast*."

She rolled her eyes, but the way they crinkled as she turned away told him there was a smile playing there. Nick followed her lead across the wide trail as she walked on and began the story.

"Faye Bartram was one of those Victorian bluestockings who did archery and bathed in hot springs and traipsed around in nature in heavy woolen outdoorsy gowns and hats and buttoned boots. Her father was a New York railroad magnate, and she was a rich spinster well into her thirties." Poppy giggled. "I guess I missed the memo on the rich part."

"I wouldn't mind seeing you in one of those Victorian archery dresses," Nick said. "Like Romola Garai wore in the BBC mini-series production of *Daniel Deronda*. But only if I get to play lady's maid. With my teeth."

Poppy's head whipped around and she bit her lip. He could spend all day teasing her.

"I can't picture you curled up with a British costume drama," she said.

He shrugged. "Good television is good television."

"Faye built the house that the Nan Fuller turned into the Damselfly Inn as a summer retreat." Poppy turned back to check that he was paying attention. "Connections."

"I'm beginning to see that."

"She would bring parties of city friends and other clever, outdoorsy types up on the train to Port Henry. They came up here and swam in this basin we're about to find. One summer when she was probably our age, but old by her own standards, she had a shocking love affair with a married Bostonian who was twenty years older. They went their separate ways at the end of the summer and he died before they could be together again. She didn't come back for years, and when she did, she was changed. She would wander the pastures at night and sail the lake in bad weather. Folks up here say she would hike out to the Hollow and call for her lover."

A shiver ran down Nick's spine. Ghost stories were the best part of late nights at summer camp in the Catskills, and he was all caught up in the legacies of this one. Something about it was familiar, though.

"Why does some of this ring a bell?"

Poppy smiled, ducking under a low branch as the trail curved and narrowed slightly. She held it long enough for him to catch it as he fell in behind her. A tantalizing glimpse of skin at the small of her back distracted him for a moment and the branch very nearly missed his hand. *That'll teach me to ogle.*

"Professor Lovatt—he's a novelist—wrote a fictionalized version of it. It hasn't been released yet, but it's getting some publicity. Maybe you saw something?"

"Probably."

"The legend is she left the cairns that mark the trail as tributes to Oscar, but I don't know…" She paused at one of the old stacks of worn stones, this one more mossy due to the thicker canopy. "I think they're just another way to mark trails. But it's romantic and sad and makes a good story."

Nick stooped to pick up a pebble from the path and left it on the cairn. If Faye and her doomed lover were still roaming the astral plane, he hoped they'd approve of his and Poppy's visit today.

CHAPTER 21

They picked up Peak Spring Brook about twenty minutes into their walk, and Poppy could hear the water tumbling into the basin in the distance. She'd forgotten that distinctive watery rush in the years since her frequent childhood visits with her father.

A silent laugh tickled her chest. Her past ahead and the near future behind her. She was a bundle of nerves, aware of Nick walking behind her with every cell in her body. Even so, it was a beautiful day, and she'd said her piece to him. True to form, Nick had put her at ease, but there was no mistaking the energy that crackled between them.

He'd left a stone on one of Faye's cairns. It was a sweet gesture, and she didn't think it was for her benefit, which only affected her more.

"We're almost there. Can you hear it?"

He stilled, eyes drifting closed in concentration. Poppy studied the planes and angles of his face. When he opened his eyes, their gazes met. Her heart thumped heavily in her chest and she let herself look at the fullness of his lower lip. Six feet between them, give or take. Enough to reduce the likelihood they were exchanging pathogens, far too much distance when what she wanted most in the world in that moment was to kiss that mouth. To wrap her arms around that man and feel his body against hers. To shed what few clothes they wore and feel the heat of skin on skin.

"Yeah," he said. His voice was raspy, rough and low.

"Just a few more minutes."

Nick cleared his throat. She thought she heard him mutter. "Or an eternity."

The continued in a charged silence as the trail rose toward the basin, the brook rambling over rocks and channeling through tree roots as it made its merry way toward the Catmint River. Its journey would take it ultimately to Lake Champlain via the Thorn River, but here in the mountains it was a child of a waterway, playful and noisy.

"Okay, 'Faye's Hollow' doesn't do this justice," Nick said. His height meant he saw over the final rock outcropping first.

About fifteen feet wide, nearly perfectly round, carved by tens of thousands of years of water pouring from one channel in the rock and swirling around before exiting via another channel at the opposite side, the deceptively deep granite bowl was full of clear, spring-fed water.

"You don't see these in the Green Mountains very often. They're more common in New Hampshire because of the way the glaciers moved through the area. The locals don't talk it up much, so you're one of us now," she said. "No telling."

He crossed his heart. "No telling. But we can just jump

in and swim? Anything I should know?"

She laughed. His expression was boyish. "It's deep in the middle, but only like a swimming pool. Not scary deep. And there are sort-of shelves arounds the sides where you can climb in and out or sit."

He reached for the back of his shirt's neck and Poppy held her breath as he hauled it over his head in that uniquely male shirt-offing way. His body was beautiful, toned and lean, but not so muscled she was afraid to want to touch. He had tan lines on his upper arms and collar. Her fingers itched to trace them.

He flashed her a wicked grin and cannonballed into the basin.

She shrieked as the mountain runoff splashed over her. Nick came up sputtering and shaking his hair like a dog.

"Jesus, that's cold." He paddled away from the middle to leave room for her. "Get in here."

Poppy cursed her insecurities as they came roaring back. Nick had been explicitly clear on the topic of his attraction, but she couldn't help but think he was used to Los Angeles bikini bodies or Long Island sailing bodies or whatever lithe sort of women guys like Nick Cooper always found themselves around.

He found himself around you, didn't he?

Nick found a shelf in the basin and used it as a seat, leaving his shoulders above water. He stretched his arms out on the ledge. "I shouldn't have said anything about the cold."

Poppy squared her shoulders and pulled the bandanna from her hair, dropping it with Nick's shirt by the side of the swimming hole. "I can take it."

Somewhere between the second and third step she shed the baggage of all the years since she'd come up here as a kid and plunged into the basin. It *was* cold, but cold like she remembered it, the memory of winter in the water, perfect after a walk through the heavy air of an unseasonably warm day. She surfaced and pushed her hair out of her eyes, seeking Nick out, wondering what harm there would truly be in going to him, in pressing their cool, slick bodies together against the rock.

They'd been so good. They'd talked about it. Two weeks seemed so arbitrary. She'd followed the rules. He'd practically been a hermit anyway, by his own admission.

She paddled backward, finding purchase on the opposite side of the basin. When she looked back at Nick, he was contemplating her, a furrow between his brows.

"What is it?"

"Just thinking," he said.

"Oh." That, in her experience, was never a good pair of words.

He must have heard it in her tone, the doubt and uncertainty that flashed over her despite his behavior. His fingers drummed the rock ledge, and his eyes traveled lazily from where her toes peeked above the surface of the water to where her chest rose from it, his gaze lingering over the vee of her neckline before coming to rest on her face. "About what it would be like to be up here with you once our lockdown is over."

Nick scooped a handful of water over his face, running his wet hand through his hair and draping his arm along the ledge.

"Would you like to hear my plans?"

She swallowed and nodded.

CHAPTER 22

"Close your eyes, Poppy." By god, when they left this basin, she would know just what power she held over him. "There's a patch of sun on your left hand. That's where I'd like to start. Can I start there?"

She nodded. Nick reveled in the sight of her, wet hair clinging to her skin, droplets scattered over her shoulders, the line of her neck exposed as she laid her head back on the ledge.

"Say the words, Poppy. Even like this, from here. I want to know what you like the sound of. I want to hear you tell me yes. I want to stop if it's not what you want."

"Yes." She stretched her left fingers. "You can start there."

"We're going to be worth every minute of this wait." He let himself weave a spell around them. "I swim in close, take your hand, stroke your palm with my thumb, taste the spot. I can't wait to find out how you taste, Beautiful."

Poppy's lashes fluttered; her fingers curled.

"Do you want to touch me?" he asked.

"So badly," she said.

"I'm so hard already. It's all for you, and we're just getting started." Nick took a breath to slow things down. "I wish I could hold you. Would you like that?"

"Yes."

"You feel so good in my arms. So right. I want to kiss you, from the hollow behind your ear where that one curl is beginning to dry, follow that drop of water down your neck, kiss along the line of that top…Would you like that?"

She nodded, then licked her lips. "Yes." Her voice cracked ever so slightly.

He knew the feeling. "I've wanted to get into your clothes for a while now. I do now. I want to slide my palms up your back, around your ribcage. I want to feel the soft skin of your breasts in my hands. But it's more than that. When you laugh, when you flirt, when you tell me your stories. I want to show you with my hands and mouth on your body what the pleasure of being with you feels like."

"Oh…"

"Is that a good, 'Oh?'"

"Yes."

Her hands drifted. One toyed with the wet hair at the nape of her neck. The other floated on the water. Nick watched her fingers for a moment, letting himself imagine the feel of those fluttering touches where he craved them most.

"Would you like it if I sat you on my lap? Do you want to feel how hard you make me?"

She whimpered slightly, lips parted, lashes fluttering,

and Nick breathed deep. Nan said they rarely saw anyone out here. Rarely wasn't never.

"I want to thread my hands in your beautiful hair and kiss you exactly the way you like to be kissed, but that means you have to kiss me first. Will you kiss me when it's time, Poppy? Show me how you like to be kissed?"

Her sigh was feather light across the water; he imagined he could feel her breath on his chest.

"Nick?" Poppy opened her eyes. They were glazed with pleasure. She was such a temptation.

"Yeah?"

"I want you to strip us both to the skin. With more than words and imagination. Not from all the way over there. I want you to make love to me. I want to trace the muscles in your forearms and run my fingers through your chest hair and suck your lower lip, and that's just what I've thought about today and while we were gardening yesterday." Her words came out in a rush. "I've never felt like this. I've never had anyone talk to me like this. I don't know how to get out of the water and put on my shoes and walk out of the woods like a person again after feeling what I just felt and we didn't even..." She blushed, the crimson stain rising hot on her chest and cheeks.

Nick wondered if that was it, if he'd just at that exact moment tumbled over a precipice and into emotions he'd assumed were meant for other people. He wondered if he would be able to exit the basin without completely embarrassing himself.

"We have a lot more *even* to do," he said, grinning to cover the wave of tenderness that threatened to swamp him, this one dwarfing the one he'd felt on the walk in. "But maybe we should stop torturing one another."

"I was torturing you?" A sly smile crept across her lips.

"You know you were," he said.

Poppy let go of the ledge and slid beneath the surface of the water. She pushed off the bottom and erupted out of the center of the basin, shaking cold water from her hair like a sprinkler.

It was his turn to shriek and laugh, but his condition, as it were, was eased—or at least distracted enough that he pushed himself up out of the water and sat on the ledge.

"Okay, fine. That's torture, too." He swung his legs up and stood, appreciating Poppy's truly luscious ass as she swam to the exit channel and climbed out.

He let her pick up her bandanna and move away to pull up her hair before he reached for his shirt, eyeballing his forearms as he did so. She liked them, did she…

He unpacked his Navajo blankets and a slightly less elegant, but far more portable lunch than their last from his pack. "Hungry?"

"Starved," she said, batting her lashes. Once again, Nick questioned his over-quick assessment of her flirting skills. He tossed her a PB&J on whole wheat, and a Ziplock baggie of granola.

Poppy caught the sandwich, but the trail mix fell next to her leg. "I didn't know you could cook."

"I haven't kept myself alive for nearly twenty years without picking up a few survival skills." He waited for Poppy to take a bite of her sandwich. When it was clear she didn't disapprove, he continued. "Like knowing that the seedless raspberry preserves get the girl every time."

"The crunchy peanut butter is a nice touch."

"You said on the phone the other night you were sad your mom didn't leave any in the pantry."

Her smile was all the reward he'd hoped for. *Pay attention, Nicolás. Girls like that*, Mariela always said.

"Where do you get your granola?"

"This is one of my secrets." He shook some out on his palm. "Mimi Marchand's cook taught me the same summer I learned about the salt marsh hay. When we can share a kitchen, I'll teach you. There's honey involved. And maple syrup."

And once again, he'd done it to himself, filled his head with visions he had no interest in banishing.

"That's just mean," Poppy said. She folded the foil from her sandwich and set it aside, along with her unfinished granola, then shifted to lie on her belly, her breasts pressed tantalizingly between her arms where she cradled her face in her palms. She crossed her ankles behind her. "I love honey. And maple syrup."

Nick reclined to one side to put a little more safety between them. They were both playing with fire today.

"Tell me about your sister," Poppy said. She dropped her arms, laying her head on them and fanning her hair out to finish drying. "Laurel, right?"

"She's great. I miss her." It was true, and the first thing to come to mind, though Nick hadn't spoken to Laurel in more than a month. "We look a lot alike, same coloring, same cheekbones. But she's tiny. Five-three."

"I'm only five-five," Poppy said.

"You're perfect," Nick replied. "Laurel and Mattie have two kids, they live outside Chicago. She's a structural engineer for a firm that specializes in rehabilitating historical structures. Mattie's a public school teacher. They met at a Polar Bear Plunge, which just proves crazy runs in the family."

Poppy's eyes had drifted closed. He watched her breathing slow. A cat nap wouldn't hurt either of them. Leaning back on his backpack, Nick let the brook's music lull him.

"Nick?" He opened his eyes to his dream girl sitting on a nearby rock snacking on her leftover granola.

"Hey." He liked waking up to her face. A lot.

"Do you want to walk the rest of the loop or go back the way we came?" she asked.

Nick sat up and scrubbed his hands through his hair.

"I want as much time with you as I can get." He wasn't going to let her earlier doubts creep in for another second, and their water play was fresh in his memory. "Do *you* want to walk the loop?"

"Yeah." Her smile was quick and true. "Let's go."

They meandered along the remaining mile and a half, drawing out the walk up Lilac lane at the end, and lingering at the split where Nick's driveway vanished into the woods. They talked about nothing and everything all at once in that way you did on the best dates. Conversations that danced and looped, moving through topics and genres and doubling back again and again until stories and histories were a tapestry of *did I tell you about?* and *you know that?*

More than once they'd drifted too near one another, their growing closeness manifesting like a magnet. Even now, as they dawdled like children, loathe to go in at the end of a long summer day, Nick noticed the careful distance they'd cultivated was shrinking.

He stepped back, doing his best not to breach the trust they were building alongside the care they were taking, much as he knew it frustrated them both.

"I'll see you tomorrow. I can come down after you're finished with work, or we could build a fire in the fire pit up at the cabin. I have to go into town for some supplies after I do my turn over at Mrs. Halladay's in the morning. I could get stuff for s'mores?"

Poppy lit up. "I haven't had a s'more since I was at a team building retreat in college."

"Deal," Nick said. "Text me when you're done with your classes and stuff."

The late afternoon sunlight pooled around them. It was light made for drugging kisses and unrushed caresses.

Nick sucked in a ragged breath. "Goodnight, Poppy."

It was a long walk up the driveway alone.

CHAPTER 23

$\mathcal{P}$oppy nearly skipped up her driveway. The melancholy and doubt that threatened the edges of her morning didn't stand a chance against Nick's relentless onslaught of sensuality and affection. She would deal with the consequences when the time came, and until then she would feast on the sheer delight of him.

She rounded the final curve, smiling at the memory of Elisha's arrival that day setting it all in motion, and her joy dried up on her lips. An airport limousine was idling in front of the house, a rangy driver with a bushy beard hanging out of his mask hauling her parents' forty-plus-year-old Samsonite luggage out of the back.

"Poppy!" She stopped in her tracks. Her father rushed around the nose of the Sprinter van, looking hale and tanned. He wrapped her in a bear hug before remembering.

"Daddy, no!" She squirmed away from him even as he dropped his arms. He smelled of spearmint gum and hand sanitizer and looked both stung and horrified. "No hugs."

"Oh, damn. I forgot." He opened the passenger's side seat of the van and left an envelope on the seat. "We got home a few hours ago. The bags were on a separate flight and they sent them along after. Very thoughtful, considering."

"Stewart!" Her mother burst through the front door, iPhone in hand. "Poppy! We were just going to start calling your cell phone. Where on earth were you?"

"Susie, she–"

"The house was all closed up. No sign of you anywhere." Her mother looked at her. "Where *have* you been?"

A lump of misery was forming behind her breastbone. She told them the truth. Minus one gorgeous, funny, definitely interested man. With each word, the wonder she'd felt with Nick slipped further away, replaced by that lump sinking slowly into her belly. "I walked out to Faye's Hollow to swim. It's quiet out there. I ate lunch. I stayed a while. I walked the loop back."

"See, Susie?" Her dad picked up two suitcases and headed in. "She was out hiking. What's safer than hiking?"

"All by herself? She could have drowned." Her mother took another suitcase and followed.

The driver shrugged, climbed into his van, removed his mask, and pulled past her, bound for the blissful freedom of not Lilac Lane. Poppy got as far as the doorway.

"Come inside, Poppy," her mother called from the front hall. "I moved your computer and put your laundry in while I got dinner started. You have done a lovely job stocking the kitchen. You can pack your things after dinner. You'll have to quarantine yourself at your apartment, I suppose, but it can't be helped, since we've had quite the trip home. How many airports, Stew?" Her mother's voice continued to drift through the house, and all Poppy could envision was a cloud of potential infection and the end of her plans to be alone together with Nick in six days. "Unless you want to stay here with us for the next two weeks?"

Her father sidled past her with a piece of carry-on luggage. "We should've called first, Pumpkin, but we got cleared to return, and the flights were arranged so quickly. We never did figure out the SIM cards…"

"It's okay, Dad," she said. "I'm just glad you're home safe."

CHAPTER 24

Nick pulled up at 1693 Bobolink Road the next morning with a head full of plans. He'd come back to the cabin to the best kind of full inbox and a next-day's agenda that included good-deed-doing and procuring Hershey bars and marshmallows.

There were emails from Sanjay about the script, but more interestingly, an email from a guy named Gabe he'd worked with back on that long-ago medical drama who was putting together a pilot program to promote and hire current, as well as educate future TV writers from marginalized populations. "Coop," the message read, "I see a place for you on the board, using your wealthy white ass connections to bring more white cash to the table. What say you?"

He liked it.

Loretta Halladay's cheerful yellow double-wide sat up close to the road. Her garden was charming and chaotic, full of whirligigs, bird feeders, plastic flamingos, gnomes, handprinted signs, glass globes, and whiskey barrels full of flowers. Nick pulled his bandanna up over his nose and hopped out of the used crossover SUV he'd picked up when he ran away to Vermont.

There was nothing in her mailbox, and no deliveries on the steps, so Nick rapped on the aluminum screen door to let her know he was around before he went to get the hose. He'd come down once before to introduce himself, so he knew it took her a moment or two to shuffle her walker from across the place, but alarm bells rang when he couldn't hear anything after a few minutes ticked by.

"Mrs. Halladay?" He banged on the metal door again. "Loretta?"

He made his way around the house, peering into windows, hoping he didn't get hauled off by some passing Sheriff for peeping on an old lady. He was around back where a deck had been gradually absorbed into a haphazard two-and-a-half season porch over the years when he saw her.

"Shit."

He dialed 911, grateful for any signal at all, given where they were. He used a high-end personal set up at the cabin to make up for the spotty service up on the mountain. "My name is Nick Cooper, I'm at sixteen-ninety-three Bobolink Road, Loretta Halladay's place. She's inside her home, lying on the floor in the ... he looked around the property... back left corner of the house. Not responding. ... I'm outside. I'm a neighbor. Here to water the flowers. Yes. I'll stay. Can I see if her doors are unlocked?"

The kitchen door was unlocked. It was run down, but clean, inside. Nick could smell weak coffee. He switched off a single-serve Mr. Coffee on the counter. "Loretta? Mrs. Halladay? You can't die on me before we've even had a chance to see if this thing is gonna work out."

Poppy, I'm sorry... This is going to put a wrench in our plans.

He found her in the back bedroom, breathing, with a thready pulse. He squatted next to her and took her hand. He thought she might have made a low, moaning noise, but it also might have been the house. "I won't lie, you're not the girl I was planning to hold hands with this week. Poppy warned me about you. She said you'd be trouble, but I didn't expect the swooning damsel gambit."

He was babbling over an unconscious octogenarian; he could feel the crisis adrenaline running its course. He wanted to cry. Instead, Nick slid down the wall behind him, holding Mrs. Halladay's limp fingers, and told her about his friend's email.

After what felt like an age, the ambulance crew arrived. He was thanked and sent on his way by the more verbal of the two paramedics. "If you're not family, there's not much we can say. Especially now. Thanks for everything you did. You probably saved her life." The medic paused as he climbed into the ambulance. "If you feel sick, you should probably get tested. I got a feeling someone will be in touch about contact tracing."

He drove back up to the cabin in a daze, stripping to the skin on the front porch, taking a scalding shower, and, after Googling where he could go for a COVID test if he needed to, giving in to sleep.

CHAPTER 25

$\mathcal{P}$oppy's apartment in Thornton was a third story walk up on the river view side of the Mercantile building. It was a spacious one bedroom with a fire escape and rooftop access, and prior to the pandemic and her idyll with Nick on Lilac Lane, it had been just about enough for her.

She hadn't taken much with her when she'd gone up to stay at her parents' house initially. Just clothes, her various creams and lotions, and the Lash Sensational for vanity's sake.

It was just housesitting. She didn't have pets or plants in town to bring her back.

Her fridge had little to offer beyond a wide range of condiments and a box of Pinot Grigio. Poppy rinsed the dust off a glass, poured herself several inches of self pity, and fell asleep in her clothes to Nick's Spotify playlist.

The unit boasted a stacking washer-dryer, which, despite her mother's best intentions the day before, Poppy put to good use as soon as she woke up. She switched on the AC, dusted, and wiped down the counters.

She was finished before Professor Bixby's first class was due to log in.

Poppy looked at her calendar with a start. There were no classes on it. The second week of June. They were finished. She had a host of meetings and paperwork to attend to, but she was free from Professor Bixby for the summer. Her first instinct was to text Nick; her phone was halfway out of her pocket when reality caught up with her. She sat down on her singleton sofa and sobbed.

It was a complicated, ugly cry, wrenched from down deep in her chest. She was relieved to have her parents safe, furious at them for ruining everything and for being selfish and thoughtless. She was angry at herself for mourning something so trivial as the sex she wasn't going to be having as soon as she was hoping for, because when it all boiled down, that was it, wasn't it?

Fat, hot tears streamed over her cheeks, soaking her shirt. She fumbled for a tissue for her streaming nose, feeling petty and small for wanting Nick so badly in the middle of a worldwide health crisis. People were dying and she was falling apart at the seams because she couldn't have a date with a guy.

But wasn't it always something? Not quite the daughter her mother wanted. Her father's work and hobbies always came out ahead, despite his best intentions. Men came and went. They didn't stay. She had a good job; she made good money. She lived in a safe, beautiful place. If she stayed, she'd get a decent retirement package. Probably. And nothing remarkable would ever happen to her.

Except…there he'd been. Something remarkable. Someone amazing. A stone's throw across Faye's Hollow, seducing her with his gilded words, doing magical things to her body without even touching her, making her laugh, treating her like someone special and calling her Beautiful and Gorgeous… and somehow she was sure, even as the tears slowed, and the snot flowed in earnest, even as the sobs became hiccups, that the magic she and Nick had stirred up was fading like a campfire left untended.

Campfire!

She was supposed to be making s'mores with him at the cabin later. She pulled out her phone again, but wasn't sure what to say.

CHAPTER 26

*N*ick woke with a pounding headache, buck naked in his bed, feeling like he'd run a marathon. The sun was high in the afternoon sky. Poppy had planned to come up for a fire and s'mores in a few hours. Such a simple plan…

The morning's events replayed for him with awful clarity while he dressed. He debated texting Poppy to tell her the news, but decided in the end that if he walked down the back way on the Horizon Trail and texted her he was there, they could at least talk in person in the wide open back yard. He'd wear two masks and make sure she stayed a lot more than six feet away from him until he found out what happened to Mrs. Halladay, but he needed to see her. He needed her to see his face, to know he wasn't blowing her off.

He set out at a brisk pace, eager to tell her everything, to get past the bad news so he could tell her how he felt. Ask her what she thought about giving them a shot. Not just *all that flirt*, but the connection they shared.

If anything, he was more sure now than he'd been the week before. He wanted to wait this thing out—however long it took—to be with her. He wanted to stay on this mountain and let his time with Poppy stretch out indefinitely. As long as it suited them both.

He wanted as much of her as she wanted to give, and you didn't tell a woman that in a text.

His phone buzzed in his pocket. He'd silenced it just before passing out.

Do you have a minute? Need to talk

Nick smiled. It was like they were tuned to each other's frequency.

Nearly to your place. Slight change of plans

Wait, Nick. Not a good idea

He cut through the hemlock grove and crossed the grass between the woods and the chicken coop. Like that not-so-long-ago day, the yellow sheets were on the line, and several of the hens were milling about scratching and picking in the tall grass along the lilac hedges. The pale gray one and her buff sister came for his feet again. He recognized the one with the flashy feathers from the night of the chocolate torte.

"Mathilda, you bad bird. Where's the sexy lady of the house?"

"Excuse me, young man. Just who are you speaking to?" Ink-dark ringlets shot through with silver under a broad straw hat followed a voice that wasn't Poppy's out from behind the sheets. He'd never asked himself what Poppy would look like in twenty or thirty years, but here was his answer. Lovely. Except for the severe expression.

"You must be Mrs. Daley," he said, leaning on a lifetime of etiquette to cover his shock. "Nick Cooper. I'm renting the Fullers' cabin up the lane." He started to offer a hand, then not only retracted it, but stepped back several feet. Not only had he had a bad morning for exposure, he realized the Daleys had been traveling internationally until very recently. So recently, in fact, that their daughter hadn't known they were coming home...

Poppy's text.

"I'm looking for Poppy."

Mrs. Daley managed to look down her nose at him from her inferior height. It was quite a trick. "I can't imagine my daughter appreciates people sneaking up on her and talking like that."

I wouldn't be so sure. "Apologies, Mrs. Daley. It won't happen again. Would you please tell her I'm here?"

"She's not here. She left last night to quarantine for fourteen days. Stewart and I are doing the same," she said pointedly, gazing at the distance between them.

"Point taken," Nick said. "I hope everything turns out okay. Be well."

Feeling helpless and a little adrift, Nick turned back toward the Horizon Trail and pulled out his phone.

CHAPTER 27

hat on earth was he doing at her parents' house?

Poppy stared at her phone, willing more information to be forthcoming, but it stayed stubbornly silent for at least five minutes. When it finally chirped, she was so jittery she nearly dropped it.

When you said not a good idea...

Her parents would chime in any minute. The man renting up the hill turning up out of the blue was too big an event to overlook, even if it hadn't had to do with her. The seed of a headache pulsed behind her left eye.

I meant not a good idea 😔 I wanted to tell you but I didn't know how
I didn't think you'd go there today

I really wanted to see your face. It was a tough morning

Sorry my parents came home and put an end to that

She typed the words out in a rush, hitting send before considering them. Her cheeks went hot. She sounded like a spoiled child. Or the bitter old spinster in one of her Regency novels.

?

She could only stare at the single punctuation mark. When she didn't reply after a few minutes, another message appeared.

Poppy? What do you mean?

She was just so tired. Tired of missing her friends. Tired of the department co-opting her position to suit the needs of a professor who couldn't be bothered learning new things. Tired of being vigilant. Tired of being alone. Tired of following the rules. Tired of craving things she couldn't have.

Maybe it was time for a clean break, even if her heart was included in it.

Two more weeks of isolating. In another week it will be something else, then something else. Eventually you'll be gone and I'll still be here. We had Faye's Hollow. Let's just keep that perfect moment and remember each other fondly

There was no reply. Not even the silly little indicator bubbles. Then her phone rang. Her mother was complaining over some kind of static before Poppy even said hello.

"Stewart, put the extension down. I'll tell you what she says." Her mother didn't actually greet her. "Poppy, who exactly is Nick Cooper?"

"I need another favor." Nick paced the cabin's front porch. The sky overhead was clear and moonless. The summer constellations wheeled overhead. It would have been a perfect night for a fire. *Fondly? Had she really used the word 'fondly?'* "I need you to help me find her."

"Nicky, slow down." Elisha's voice was tinny over the poor cell signal. "What do you need?"

"Poppy Daley. Her address. I Googled, but her public listings go back to her parents' place here on Lilac Lane."

"Isn't that where she is?"

Nick stopped pacing long enough to press his forehead against the cabin wall. Fireflies blinked from the edge of the clearing, calling to one another in the darkness. "A lot happened since I sent her those sexy croissants you suggested."

"So I gather."

"She works for the history department at the college.

She's an administrative assistant. Can you find out where she lives?"

There was a long pause during which Nick began pacing again.

Elisha finally spoke with measured care. "Does she want you to find her?"

"We've been spending a lot of time together. Responsibly. And we had this plan to be decidedly less responsible at the end of two weeks"

Elisha let out a ladylike snort.

Nick didn't let her derail him. "Everything went sideways in the last twenty-four hours and it's like something broke down. She's giving up. I have to talk to her. I don't want her to give up on us."

"You never do things by halves."

He pushed his fist against a porch support. "Are you going to help me?"

"I'll see what I can do," Elisha said. "Nicky, you sound a little rough around the edges. Whatever plan you're hatching, sleep on it."

"Yeah."

"I mean it," Elisha said.

Nick heard the stern warning and dropped into the nearest chair, regretting it immediately, as it conjured memories of Poppy turning up with cookies and gin.

"Do you remember when you thought Jameson Connelly stood your sister up for her winter formal and you locked him in the elevator machine room?"

Nick laughed, remembering the screw up. He'd definitely gone off half cocked to defend Laurel's honor. "And she was out dancing the night happily away with Jamie's sister who went to Saint Brigit's? Fine. I'll sleep on it."

Elisha pulled out her ace. "Mariela would be proud. I'll text you."

The frantic energy dissipated somewhat, and Nick realized he'd barely eaten all day. He was halfway through a pan of scrambled eggs and toast twenty minutes later when Elisha texted an address.

1 Mercantile apt 3A. Next time you're in Newport, you have to stop and have a meal with Mimi and Grand-père. x

Nick sincerely hoped he'd have the opportunity to go to Newport in the near future. If he got what he wanted, he'd bring a plus-one.

Consider it done x

He did sleep on it, and woke up a man on a mission. He brewed a pot of coffee, opened his laptop and a legal pad and set out to win Poppy Daley back from a responsible social distance.

First stop, those croissants. The bakery answered on the second ring. It was odd to think that the rest of Vermont was starting to reopen just as he and Poppy were locking down again, and farther apart than ever.

"Sweet Pease Patisserie and Café."

"Hi," he said, liking the whiskey and sugar voice on the other end of the line. "I'd like to place a delivery order."

"Something specific, or one of our gift baskets?"

"A half dozen chocolate croissants, as soon as they are able be delivered."

"I've got those in stock now. Downtown, I can send a courier today. Otherwise, tomorrow. Anything else?"

"That's it. And she's in the Mercantile. Can you do it at a specific time?"

"Within reason. I'll need an address and a credit card. Do you want to include a message with the delivery?"

Nick heard the smile in the question. "Yeah, can you add, 'No matter what you've heard, we'll be better'?"

"No name?"

"She'll know."

"I hope so." That smile in the voice again.

He gave her the info, and moved on to his next call. A florist on the next block called Josephine's. The owner not only answered but was willing to help him with his plans. Nick was immediately smitten with CeCe Drexler.

"What do you know about the language of flowers, young man?"

"Less than you think," he said.

She laughed. "So much sass. Pink camellias signify longing. I grow one that looks more like a peony, and I happen to think they are a very *sensual* flower. I can see the Mercantile building from my shop. I'll have a bowlful delivered within the hour."

"You're an angel. Someday when this is all over, I'm going to come in there and kiss you."

"Save them for your lady friend, Romeo."

It was amazing what a little extra cash could accomplish. While CeCe ran his card, he logged into Spotify and added a few new tracks to Poppy's playlist, hoping she might still give it a listen and hear what he was trying to tell her.

When he called the Thornton Co-op Market, he spoke

with an older woman who obviously knew nothing about wine, but was happy to sell him a selection of bottles from a local vineyard that shared his name, and send a runner to have them delivered to Poppy's apartment at the right time. In that six minute call, he learned more about her daughter's recommendations on wine and local eateries than he could have from Yelp. As he had with his previous purchases, Nick added a generous tip and made a note to call his dad. He owed his present solvency solely to his father's insistence that he invest wisely when there was money to do so.

He could learn to like this small town thing.

Next up: email Gabe to follow up and connect him with Sanjay to recruit him to teach and mentor. Grant writing, fund-raising and glad-handing meant he could base himself anywhere, meaning right here. Then an email to the moderator of Loretta Halladay's care group to see what he could find out and make sure his future shifts were covered for a few weeks while he stayed out of everyone's way.

He was humming The National's *Slow Show* as he opened the FedEx envelope that arrived while he was on the phone. Margot's goodwill meant favors. Favors meant an ARC of Ewan Lovatt's new novel, a fictionalized history of New York railroad heiress Faye Bartram and her scandalous and tragic love affair with Boston Brahmin Oscar Pinckney less than a year before his untimely death.

With any luck, he could get through a few chapters before the flowers would arrive at Poppy's apartment, kicking off the cascade of gifts that meant Nick had somewhere very important to be.

CHAPTER 29

Poppy woke determined to put Nick behind her. He'd obviously taken her suggestion at face value. She refused to admit to herself that it surprised–and destroyed–her how easily he'd accepted her goodbye.

Even the recently-destroyed needed more than rice wine vinegar, chili garlic paste, dijon mustard, olives, some old cereal, and sad, singleton pantry staples to survive. She put in a curbside pickup order for groceries from the chain store a few miles south of town and made coffee to clear her head.

She met with the rest of the administrative team via screens to map out getting the cloud filing completed for the previous semester and ready for grading. Scheduling would have to wait until the college settled on a plan for the fall semester. With summer learning suspended, she would have a light work load until the department catalog and website needed to be updated and the students and majors brought up to speed for whatever awaited them.

She was facing about two weeks of simple clerical work, when what she knew she needed was an outright deluge of projects.

Over her lunch, she pinged Nisha and Meg, hoping her besties could offer some wisdom.

"Girl. We let you skip *one* brunch, and this is what you get up to?" Nisha worked as a hospitality coordinator for a ski area, which usually meant summers spent at brewfests and mountain bike rallies and outdoor concerts. This summer, she was collecting what unemployment she could and living in pajama pants, perfecting the art of the two-pencil bun. Today, she had hot pink Hello Kitty pencils sticking out of her topknot. "Honestly, though. What's the big deal? Maybe he won't care about your parents' exposure if it means boning? Bet if you text him some nudes he'd stop feeling all wounded and come around."

"Yeah, no," Poppy said.

Meg rolled her eyes. "Neenee, he obviously takes this seriously. He proposed the two-week isolation to start. Honey, I think you did the right thing." She cradled a chunky pottery mug between her hands. Poppy figured the AC in Meg's condo was cranked down to 68°. "I know it hurts right now, but he's clearly got stuff of his own to work through or he wouldn't have run away to Catmint Gap in the first place."

"You two are a lot of help," Poppy muttered.

"You already blew him off," Nisha said. "We're just offering commentary."

"I have a product meeting in five. Gotta jet," Meg said. "Check in later, okay? Don't wallow."

Meg's square winked out. Nisha shrugged. "I love you,

girl. But I think you need to get *laaaiiiiiid*, and I Googled your Nick Cooper. I'd have held out to tap that coronavirus-free ass, is all I'm saying."

Poppy sighed. "It's just hard to believe he'd have held out for me."

"Difficult to say, based on the information provided." Nisha leaned in close to her laptop screen. "You gave him a test that was impossible to pass. And Meg's right. Don't wallow."

Poppy's phone rang, freeing her from Nisha's uncomfortable insight. She hadn't heard her ringtones so frequently since the world shut down back in March. Which meant, of course, it was one of her parents.

"Hi, Daddy. What's up?"

"I just got off the phone with Dawn down at the market in the village. I phoned in a curbside pickup order." He sounded inordinately proud of himself.

"Okay."

"Did you hear that Loretta Halladay is in the hospital? Dawn said she was taken by ambulance yesterday morning."

"No, that's awful." Poppy tucked her phone between her cheek and shoulder, and closed her Zoom app to open her browser. Time to check the neighborhood group for updates."What happened?"

"Someone found her unconscious in her house and called the ambulance. No one knows yet, but it could be the coronavirus. Were you over there at all? Dawn says folks are starting to worry that her visiting nurse might have it."

Poppy took a deep breath through her nose. "No,

Daddy. I only chatted with her from the driveway, through her window while I was watering her flowers."

"That's a relief, Pumpkin," he said. "You left a note on my desk, maybe a bakery order. It says, "French kiss cupcake?' Sounds racy. Something from that place in town?"

Thank god they don't FaceTime. Her face betrayed everything. "Nothing important, Daddy. You can toss it."

Her father finished updating her on other Catmint Gap news she wasn't interested in, then ended the call to answer her mother's summons.

Poor Mrs. Halladay. Which of the neighborhood volunteers had been there to find her? The Facebook group was all aflutter, but sifting through the posts was frustrating since word was indeed spreading about the home health aide's possible infection. When it hit her, she felt like a prize idiot. Nick, standing in the slanted, filtered sunlight at the point where Lilac Lane ended and their driveways began, the point where, had they been less cautious, they might have chosen to walk down one of those driveways together.

Into one of two *very* different evenings.

I have to go into town for some supplies after I do my turn over at Mrs. Halladay's in the morning.

I really wanted to see your face. I had a tough morning.

Oh, Nick.

Her doorbell buzzer rang. She wound her way around her discarded shoes and tote bags to press the intercom button, a charming reminder of the last time the building had had any significant updates. "Hello?"

"Delivery for Poppy Daley?" The voice sounded young and muffled.

"This is she."

"Flowers from Josephine's. I'm leaving them on the table in the lobby. If you verbally accept them, you don't have to sign anything. New rules. Have a good day."

"Okay, sure." She waited a moment, letting her racing heart and shaking hands have a moment.

Flowers.

She put on a mask and took the stairs as quickly as she dared. There, on the antique sideboard that occupied one entire wall of the dated lobby, was a wide, shallow ceramic bowl of ruffly pink flowers. They practically erupted out of the bowl, pushing one another out of the way to be noticed, showy and lush. A small gray card was staked into the arrangement.

She picked it up with trembling fingers.

Inside was a typed note.

    Far more than fondly. N.

She was still studying the letters when a young woman in a babydoll dress and combat boots, with long mermaid hair on one side of her head and a turquoise fade on the other, wearing a fuchsia mask bearing the Sweet Pease logo pushed the lobby door open. She was carrying a pastry box tied with string in one hand and a tablet in the other.

"Do you live here?" she said.

"I do. Who are you looking for?" Poppy answered.

The mermaid checked her screen. "Poppy Daley, apartment 3A."

"You found her. I didn't order anything, though."

"That's the name, though." She used a wipe to sanitize

the screen then held out the tablet. "I need a signature. Just a scrawl or whatever." She set the pastry box on the table next to the flowers. "Those are gorgeous. Camellias, right? I took a class at Josephine's last winter on the language of flowers. I forget which color means what, but like, one is for someone you adore, one means desire, and one is for someone you long for. It's crazy romantic. I never knew. Anyway, whoever does your lobby has great taste. Enjoy your croissants."

Mermaid Girl was gone as quickly as she'd come. Poppy untied the box and unfolded the note threaded into the twine.

No matter what you've heard, we'll be better.

Poppy recognized Kate Pease's handwriting from years of departmental invoices, but she knew Nick's words when she read them. The way they'd flirted on his front porch was seared across her heart.

Inside the box were six chocolate croissants. Her stomach rumbled just thinking about them.

Between the flowers and the pastries, she was going to have to use the elevator.

When the lobby doors opened again, she almost laughed. The residential entry of the Mercantile never saw this kind of non-resident traffic, even pre-pandemic. This time, a bald, middle-aged man in a polo shirt, apron from the Co-op, and a New England Patriots mask with a player number on one side wheeled in a dolly carrying a case of wine. From Cooper Vineyards. Of course. Nick was everywhere all of a sudden.

"Going up?" Poppy asked, ready to cede the elevator.

"Third floor. Apartment 3A."

"Really?" she said. "Daley?"

"That's the one," he said.

"That's me." Her head was spinning. Why was Nick going to all this trouble now? "Would you do me a huge favor and take the flowers and this box up on your dolly in the elevator? I'll meet you on the third floor and take everything inside."

"Sure I can take everything up, but I got a message to deliver to Poppy first. That you, too?"

"It is."

The courier pulled a piece of lined paper from his apron pocket and cleared his throat. "'The way I see it, Poppy, I have twelve days to show you how much you mean to me. Neat coincidence that each of these twelve bottles has my name on it. PS: you never told me you had a roof deck.'"

Roof deck? Roof deck. Nick.

She ran for the stairwell door.

"Miss? Your stuff?"

"Just leave it all outside 3A, please. Thank you!" She dashed up the stairs, sucking air against the mask in her effort to get to the roof faster.

She fumbled with her key as the elevator rumbled up behind her. She was inside and unlocking her roof access stairs when the elevator door dinged in the corridor outside.

She burst through the creaky steel door, pulling the mask down to breathe in some fresh air after four flights of stairs. She hadn't been out here for months. The shared roof was divided among the third floor tenants by lattice half-walls, making four unique terraces. Hers boasted a door directly to her unit. The other three used the fire escape.

And that was where she found him, sitting with his back against the fire escape railing, waiting for her to arrive.

He stood, staying where he was, keeping his bandanna up over his nose, but it couldn't hide the crack in his voice. "Hey, Gorgeous. What's up?"

CHAPTER 30

*N*ick had run through this moment a hundred times since he'd cooked up his plan to win her back, but he hadn't accounted for her running up four flights of stairs in a face mask on a hot day.

He hadn't realized how beautiful the sight of her, out of breath and a little red in the face, would be.

"I can't believe you did all that—"

"I'll wait all summer, it doesn't matter—"

The both laughed. Poppy pushed her mask back up and leaned against a duct. He let her catch her breath.

"Loretta Halladay had some kind of collapse the other morning. I found her when I went to check on her flowers," he began.

"I know, I only heard this morning from my dad—"

"I went inside her house because I had to make sure she was…well, I couldn't just leave her in there alone and possibly frightened, but knowing I was ruining our plans, Poppy, it hurt. And I hurt knowing I was going to disappoint you…"

"Nick, I—"

"And then I crashed for a bit, and realized I'd forgotten our s'mores date, so I went down to your place—your parents' place—to tell you face to face so you'd know, really know, how it affected me. But also, because there were other things I'd realized. Other things I wanted to say."

Poppy groaned. "And instead you found my parents."

"You can grow up to look like your mom any day. She's a bit of a silver fox."

"Oh, my god. Shut up."

Nick grinned when she scolded him. Her bubbling laugh released some of the anxious energy that swirled between them.

"So we both had a wrench thrown in our plans. And maybe you're right, maybe in another week there will be something else. But maybe we both get a test, and we see what happens. That's not the part that matters to me."

Poppy pulled her knees up and wrapped her arms around them. "No?"

She looked so vulnerable; it would all be so much simpler to go to her, wrap her up in his arms, bury his face in the warmth of her hair and whisper what was happening in his heart. Instead, they had this, a bright, warm June afternoon on a roof by a river, both worried about exposure they didn't bring upon themselves.

And it would have to be enough.

"When we fell asleep at Faye's Hollow the other day, I liked waking up to your face. I liked making plans with you. To help in the garden or have a picnic. The idea of tomorrow was starting to mean plans with you. That's what I want: for tomorrow to always mean plans with you."

He stopped, letting those words rest on the air, watching her reaction. Her eyes were shining, but she didn't speak.

"I won't lie, Poppy. I want to touch you. Badly. But I think this stopped being just about the physical payoff a while ago. I want to plan more hikes and trips to the farmer's market, I want to stay in bed and make love all day. I want to take you to Scotland to bag a Monroe, even if I'm still not sure exactly what that means or if I'll need a safe word. I don't care how long it takes to clear this quarantine as long as you're in my arms at the end of it."

He took a deep breath, conjuring the magic from Faye's Hollow and meeting Poppy's gaze across the roof terrace.

"Tell me, because I want to hear you say the words, would you like that?"

She released her knees, pressing her hands against the worn tar and gravel surface. "Yes."

TWELVE DAYS LATER

*N*ick was enjoying an excellent shower fantasy involving Poppy in her polka dot halter top and the matching bikini bottom she'd finally admitted to owning when they went kayaking on Lake Champlain when brisk knocking on the cabin door interrupted.

"Jesus, what now?" *You join one neighborhood group and suddenly people start turning up, even in phase two of the state's reopening.* One day it was someone canvassing for a local special election, one day it was Loretta Halladay's out-of-town family stopping to leave a thank-you gift. The elder Daleys regularly came up to leave eggs on the porch, having been given a serious talking-to by their daughter.

The same daughter who was expected at the cabin after she finished a day of online department meetings regarding the college's fall semester learning strategies, followed by filing visa paperwork for some international history majors, and sweet mother of arousal did his body know it. His showers had grown progressively colder all week.

In honor of the Daleys' delicious daughter's impending arrival, he grabbed his Columbia Prep flannels from the hook on the bathroom door and toweled his freshly trimmed hair on the way to the door.

"Hi—" Nick flung open the door expecting anyone but the woman who stood there, wearing the wraparound dress he'd liked so much in her parents' backyard. "Poppy?"

She waited at the bottom of the stairs, a reasonable distance away, still unreasonably tempting, given the big red circle around the date in his imagination.

"Why do I feel like we've been here before?" She was smiling, bouncing on the balls of her feet like a kid with a secret.

"What's going on?"

"I didn't tell you because I didn't want to get our hopes up, but I got tested the other day through work. After you said that Mrs. Halladay was just dehydrated and her health aide didn't have it, I thought, why not? Right?" She was practically glowing. "But then the results took a few days, so it wasn't going to matter. And then last night I got an email and no antibodies, which is good, right?"

Nick's pulse thrummed. She needed to come up those stairs soon or he was likely to combust. "Definitely right."

"So I called in sick." She reached into the tote bag he only now noticed she was carrying and revealed the neck of the last bottle of Cooper Vineyards wine. She batted her eyelashes and grinned. "Wanna play hooky with me? I thought we could—"

He was down the stairs and gathering her against him before she could squeak out another teasing word. The bag and bottle thumped to the ground. For a long moment they clung to one another, basking in the sweetness of touch so long denied. The sensory overload took his breath away: silky curls and satin skin against his chest, her warm breath, the damp spots where his still wet skin soaked through her dress, her heartbeat.

He'd missed contact. To finally have it with her was almost unbearably wonderful.

She leaned back in his embrace to look up at him. "By your lips. That's how I'd like to be kissed."

"Never been so glad to oblige."

He stroked the dusting of freckles on her cheek with his thumb, leaning in to chase the touch with his mouth, feathering kisses over her face until her lips parted in breathless invitation. She smoothed her hands over his bare shoulders.

"You're shaking," she said softly.

"I want to get this right."

"Kiss me, Nick. Then let's make some plans."

They came together, a crushing, tangling, hungry kiss weeks in the making. Poppy tightened her arms around his neck, stretching up on her toes. Nick scooped her up and she wrapped her legs around his waist, laughing against his lips as he made his way backward to sit on the stairs.

He paused for a breath, leaning his forehead against hers. "Worth it."

She took his face in her hands. He hadn't gotten to shaving yet when she interrupted his shower, and her palms rasped his day's beard growth. "I like this. I don't usually see you first thing in the morning."

Nick growled low and nipped at her lips. "I'd like to remedy that. Tomorrow morning. Starting now."

Poppy climbed off his lap, giving him a generous glimpse of pale thigh. She retrieved her bag and started up the cabin stairs, trailing a finger along his arm. "How did you phrase it just now? 'Never been so glad to oblige.'"

A NOTE FROM THE AUTHOR

This story, originally titled *Alone Together on Lilac Lane*, appeared in online serial form this past summer, exclusively for my newsletter subscribers. It started as a way to reboot my creativity after a long, dark spring.

Like a lot of us, in March I found myself suddenly quarantining with my family, unsure of how long school was going to be done from a distance, how my husband's work was going to go, how my day jobs would weather the storm.

I tinkered with a few works-in-progress, but contemporary romance seemed a million miles away with emerging science telling us that lingering embraces with anyone but our housemates wasn't going to fly. Honestly, I couldn't even watch commercials without thinking, "Where are their masks?"

I kept asking myself, can romance happen despite masks and social distancing? What would that even *look like?*

Finally, what it came down to was this: *if you can't ignore the pandemic, write about it.*

I guess it helps that I think anticipation is sexy as hell.

If you've read the Thornton novels, I hope you enjoyed the easter eggs. And speaking of easter eggs, eBook readers: when Nick says he made Poppy *something*, there's a Spotify link there for you, too.

If you enjoyed getting to know a few of the residents of Catmint Gap, I hope you'll take a chance on neighboring Blueberry Hill, and keep an eye out for the Green Mountain Hearts trilogy, coming in April 2021 (or before if you know where to look).

Here's to a new year and new possibilities!

Cheers, Cameron
December 2020

PS–Turn the page for a sneak peek at AMBITIOUS HEART, book one of the upcoming Green Mountain Hearts series.

AMBITIOUS HEART

CHAPTER ONE

There were few things Marnie Burnham loved more than a bluebird day in January, when a fresh flurry sugared the week-old slush and the late afternoon sun gilded the frosted mountains that stood sentry over the village of Blueberry Hill.

The second Thursday of January in 2002 was going to the top of her list. Not only were the makings of a storybook sunset assembling over the far distant Adirondacks, but she'd spent the cloudless day on the slopes with her dad, testing out the new Burton demo board he'd gotten in at the pro shop, and tonight…Tonight, after a hundred years, the lease on the Blueberry Hill Grange Hall expired, and per town ordinance, the board of selectmen could redesignate the property for public use.

Marnie Burnham had a plan.

She dodged a patch of ice, tightening her grip on the sheaf of paperwork tucked under her arm. Her iBook was fully charged, ready to plug into the projection system she'd borrowed from the Thornton College tech library. If she was using a bedsheet as a display, well, Truman Bixby and the rest of the board would just have to excuse her lack of professional presentation equipment.

Her phone rang, and Marnie stopped to perch on the bench outside Karly's Klips while she took the call. The name on the display brought a smile to her face.

"Sam!" Marnie tucked the phone between her cheek and sat on the file folders to keep them from blowing away. "I got your email earlier. How was the first day of subbing? Those kids don't know how lucky they are."

"I'm the lucky one." Samantha Ellis was her oldest friend. Oldest and farthest away. Sam was at Tulane getting a masters in education, and in Marnie's opinion, not seeing nearly enough live jazz. "The kids are great, my graduate program is great, and I'm volunteering through a charitable foundation sponsored by the Lacroix family, which is kind of a big deal."

"You know what else is a big deal?" Marnie grinned, winding up for a well-used inside joke.

"Live music in New Orleans," Sam said with a sigh. "I know. I promise. Maybe I'll ask Craig to go with me."

"Did you just bury a man-lede on the second Thursday of January in 2002?" Marnie resisted the urge to shriek. Selectman Bixby was a block away headed for the town offices. "I wish you could be here tonight to watch me convince that bunch of fossils to give the one-woman Blueberry Hill Farmer's Market Committee the Grange Hall…right before I grill you about *Craig*."

"I'm sure you won't forget to do that as soon as it's over," Sam said. "And I wish I could be there, too. Now go set up your magic. I love you, crazy lady."

Marnie was about to hang up the call when a shiny

mid-size pickup with New York plates growled to a stop outside Video Visions and more than six well-filled-out feet of Viking-meets-surfer dropped down from the driver's side.

"I'm going, but before I do, let me say that a Toyota Tacoma just parked outside Jim Dix's video store like he owned the place, and I'm thinking about including myself as a rider on the contract, if you know what I mean."

Sam's laugh was loud enough through the phone that the surfer Viking turned in Marnie's direction, catching her in the act of checking him out. His face was in shadow, but she got the impression of a strong profile, and holy hell, he wore glasses. Seriously sexy frames and a low, not-too-long ponytail of dirty blond hair; a body built for pillaging dressed in a crisp button down and wool pants that fit like they'd been tailored.

Who was this guy and what on earth was he doing in Blueberry Hill, Vermont?

"Helloooooo? Marnie," Sam said, maybe for the second or third time. "I'm hanging up. I love you. Good luck!"

"Thanks, Sam. Talk soon!" Marnie flipped her phone shut and shoved it toward the bottom of her bag, sucking in a lungful of cold air to clear her head. She had a room of selectmen and townsfolk to wow.

What Marnie lacked in resources, she more than made up for in passion and forward thinking. Her mother's homemade soaps and cleaning products flew out of the baskets and bins in the refurbished pop-up trailer she towed around to county fairs all summer. Local folks knocked on the Burnhams' back door, and the general store over in Catmint Gap sold out weekly. The Beasleys' honey was legendary as far south as the Deerfield Fair, and any number of veggie patches and chicken coops around town traded and sold goods between neighbors in their foothills hamlet.

All across the state, farmers markets were cropping up and expanding like wild mushrooms. Blueberry Hill was near a major ski area, a good-sized college town, and the Appalachian trail, and there were a bunch of local farms, orchards, and crafters around who could anchor a diverse market. The kind of market that could support a micro-economy if it ran year-round, and where better to run year round than in the Blueberry Hill Grange Hall, a wide open indoor space that would belong to the town as of midnight.

"Marnie!"

Marnie spun around to find her mother rushing down the sidewalk, a cloud of scarves and graying curls floating around her face like a corona in the sunset.

"Hey, Mama Llama, you ready?"

"I slipped into the town meeting room earlier this afternoon and worked a little charm for favorable outcomes, I have samples in a basket to leave near the door and some notes for my testimonial–" Daphne Potter caught Marnie's brewing interruption and cut her off. "No love potions in the shampoo, promise, and I won't even bring up that I'm your mother. Did you wear your sapphires?"

Marnie sighed and touched the sapphire chip earrings her parents gave her for her sixteenth birthday. "Because they're the nicest ones I have, Mom."

"They're lucky." Her mother *tsk*'d. "You have magic in your blood, Marnie. All the Potter women have it. You shouldn't knock it 'til you try it."

"I'm a Burnham, Mom."

Her mother muttered something about the patriarchy as she drifted past her on a bergamot scented cloud, patting Marnie's cheek as she passed.

It took twenty minutes to hang up the white sheet, find a suitable place to set up the projector and get her iBook connected. She tested her PowerPoint slideshow, went through her notes, and fidgeted with her dress's hem. The straight sheath style with the short–but not too short–skirt was the most adult thing she owned, bought for job interviews after college a few years before. She'd debated showing up in her usual uniform of thrift store flannel, bootcut jeans, and Bean boots, but she wanted the board to take her seriously.

It was an eternity waiting through the shuffling of seats, the reading of minutes, and the discussion of a minor change to the dog licensing bylaws. Finally, Truman Bixby announced the matter of the Grange Hall lease.

"The terms of the Pinckney estate stipulate that we must hear proposals for the use of the hall prior to the close of the hundred-year Grange Hall lease period. The town will then choose, at the discretion of the board of selectmen, which proposal to grant the next lease period to and for how long. If no feasible proposal is offered, the land reverts to the town to dispose of as it sees fit."

Tom Crawford hefted his portly frame out of his chair and announced the Blueberry Hill Farmer's Market Committee. Marnie ignored the smattering of laughter from the assembled crowd as she walked to the front of the room.

"Good evening, Selectman Bixby, Selectman Crawford, the assembled board, friends, neighbors." She paused to snatch a breath and squeeze her fingers together to quell her anxiety. "I'm fairly certain I know everyone here, but I'll introduce myself anyway." Her gaze fell on the Viking surfer from New York, as if on cue. He sat in the third row, his hair gilded by the terrible overhead lighting in the meeting room, his expression carefully neutral. He did have a strong profile, but a gentle mouth, with laugh lines, or maybe too-much-time in-the-sun lines. "I'm Marnie Burnham, founder of the Blueberry Hill Farmer's Market Committee, and I propose the Grange Hall be turned into a year-round open market for regional crafters, farmers, and artisans to create a local micro-economy that serves both community interests and tourism demands. If you'll all indulge me, I've prepared a short presentation."

As she spoke the jittery nerves melted away. The technology actually behaved, and the presentation went off without a hitch. Even her mother, with her hippie folk magic vibe, managed to stay on message, and people around town did love the soaps.

"Thank you all for your time. I hope you'll consider this proposal to enrich our community in spirit and in commerce."

She took her seat, and let her hands and feet shake the way they'd wanted to for the last twenty minutes.

Arlene Levesque stood, prim and formal as she'd been twenty years before when she'd taught Marnie's Kindergarten class. "The number of proposals submitted in advance was a matter of public record. We had planned to hear three tonight, but the two remaining have withdrawn, citing financial reasons." Arlene's brow creased slightly as she surveyed the room. "If there is anyone in the audience this evening with a proposal to add, we will hear it now, otherwise I think I speak for the board when I say Marnie Burnham's passion for the marketplace certainly grants her at least a short term lease to try the idea out."

Marnie's heart flipped over in her chest and she bit her lip to keep from letting her joy get the better of her volume control. There was no way anyone in the room would take this away from her. Not now.

"Excuse me, Madame Selectman, members of the board." The Viking surfer stood, tugging at his cuffs and clearing his throat. "My name is Micah Reynolds, representing Simmons-Doyle Development of Albany. My firm is prepared to buy the property outright at 110% of market value for the development of a boutique micro-hotel property, should the board decide not to grant a lease."

Marnie's pulse slowed and the floor seemed to fall away beneath her, even as she straightened her spine and stared the handsome stranger down for the second time that day. This time, she didn't see a long-legged, seafaring god. The man who'd just offered the town a fortune in exchange for her dream resembled nothing so much as a flint-eyed marauder.

Bread & Promises (Wish)

The Soloist (Joy)

Star of Wonder (Merry Little Christmas)

Santa's Photographer (Secret Santas)

Merry's Christmas (Atlantic to Pacific)

Twelve Days 'til Christmas

CHILDREN OF THE PARALLELS

SPECULATIVE MIDDLE GRADE SHORT FICTION

Parallel Jump

Parallel Hunt

ACKNOWLEDGMENTS

Thank you to everyone who helped me get this book out of my computer and into the world:

Ko-fi supporters Ashley and Alonza, I see you!
Patti & Lawrence: best Quaranteam ever!
My husband and son, more than ever my mostly companions and true believers.
Sebastian Malloy, my madman in a box.
The Bad Bird Brigade: Flüf, Giraffe, Trudy, and Sharpie– the chickens who inspired the Daleys' flock

and lastly, because it is impossible that I should get anything done without them, *always* Mandy Dawson and Angela Amman, the best writing friends a gal could ever have.

ABOUT THE AUTHOR

Cameron D. Garriepy attended a small Vermont college in a town very like Thornton. She's missed it since the day she packed up her Subaru and drove off into the real world. Some might say she created the fictional village as wish fulfillment, and they would be correct.

She is the author of the Thornton Vermont series, and the founder of Bannerwing Books, a co-op of independent authors. Prior to Bannerwing, Cameron was an editor at Write on Edge, where she curated three volumes of the online writing group's literary anthology, Precipice. Cameron appeared in the inaugural cast of Listen to Your Mother – Boston, and irregularly contributed flash fiction to the Word Count Podcast.

Since her time at Middlebury College, Cameron has worked as a camp counselor, nanny, pastry cook, an event ticket resale specialist, and an office manager. Cameron's ghost-writing and editing hides in the tech and finance sectors. In her spare time, she is an archer, a baker, a gardener, a knitter, and a reader of a lot of romance novels.

Cameron writes from the greater Boston area, where she lives with her husband, son, and four naughty hens. They are all awaiting the arrival of a pug puppy under the Christmas tree.

Connect with Cameron online at www.
camerondgarriepy.com
Hear first about sales and new releases via Cameron's
newsletter—subscribe at
bit.ly/smartsexynewsletter
Join the conversation in Cameron's Facebook group at
bit.ly/thorntonfbgroup

amazon.com/author/camerondgarriepy

facebook.com/camerondgarriepy

twitter.com/camerongarriepy

goodreads.com/camerondgarriepy

bookbub.com/authors/cameron-d-garriepy

instagram.com/camerongarriepy

pinterest.com/camerongarriepy

ABOUT THE PUBLISHER

Bannerwing Books is a writers' co-op founded in 2012 by Cameron D. Garriepy, and completed by Angela Amman and Mandy Dawson. Currently residing on Slack, somewhere in the ether between Boston, Detroit, and Paso Robles, Bannerwing presents works by Stephanie Ayers, Ericka Clay, and Liz Zimmers, as well as collections featuring Andra Watkins, Kate Shrewsday, and Kameko Murakami.

www.bannerwingbooks.com

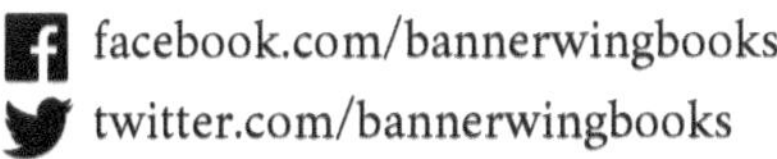

facebook.com/bannerwingbooks
twitter.com/bannerwingbooks

BUCK'S LANDING

AN EXCERPT

CHAPTER 1

Whoever was pounding on the door had better have their affairs in order, Sofia thought as she pushed herself up off the sofa, because she was going to murder them with her bare hands. With a grimace at the empty bottle of pinot noir on the coffee table, she cursed herself for drinking too much the night before, pressing her knuckles against her sleep-crusted eyes. Hadn't she fled this coastal New England beach town to escape her father's drinking? She scraped her mane of dark brown curls into a hasty knot, wondering what the hell else a lone woman was expected to do in Hampton Beach when she wasn't one of the vacationing hordes.

A glance at the clock told her she'd overslept. The mini-golf course at Buck's Landing would be open by now, and she should be getting the Snack Bar ready.

She opened the door to Amy, her assistant manager. The coed's perky ponytail and crisp uniform polo shirt practically sparkled in the July sun.

"I'm sorry, Sofia." Amy glanced down from Sofia's third story landing at the Astroturf greens, where a small crowd had gathered around the cement "tree" on the twelfth hole. "There's a kitten stuck up the tree, and I can't get him down."

"Of course." With a sigh, Sofia slid her feet into the sensible sport sandals she wore to work, and followed Amy down the stairs to the waiting cat. She praised herself for falling asleep in a tank top and soft cotton pants. At least she was decent enough to rescue stray kittens from fake cement trees.

The sun glittered off the crushed stone paths that wound through the course, sparkled on the blue-gray sea washing ashore across the street at the state beach. Heat was already pooling on the sidewalk, the boardwalk, and the road between. Sofia squinted, wishing for sunglasses, and did her best to ignore the faint throbbing at her temple.

A six-foot ladder proved enough to get her into the tree, and the little scrap of fur came to her easily. Sofia had never had a cat, but as this kitten's body went soft in her hands, she wondered briefly why not.

"Aren't you a pretty...well, now what are you?" She raised the tiny cat up and inspected its underside. "A pretty boy." He cocked his head to one side, and Sofia chuckled. She tucked the purring feline under her arm and backed down the ladder. "Amy, can you stash the ladder on your way back to the window? I'm going to find a place for this guy to stay until I find his owner."

"Sure."

Sofia envied the college girl's boundless energy. She hadn't remembered having that much buoyant charm at twenty-two. All she remembered about being a college kid was planning her summers off from UNH so that she could be home as little as possible. The summer she was twenty-two, she'd worked her third consecutive summer at a girls' camp in the White Mountains, blessing them for providing room and board. She'd stashed her paychecks away, saving for the precious future, intent on escaping her father's grief and its companion, Canadian whiskey. She had planned to get out of New England, alone.

She carried the kitten up to the landing outside her apartment. Below her, Hampton's Ocean Boulevard was already awake and bustling. Salt and sand seasoned the breeze blowing in off the water. Motels, restaurants, food counters, and seaside souvenir shops lined the sidewalk of the boulevard as far as she could see before the coastline curved eastward at Rocky Bend. She smoothed out the cat's long tail while her eye traced the farthest point where the year-round colony sat on the bluff.

Buck's Landing sat amongst all the tourist traps, three stories high and half a block wide in every direction. Her grandfather had designed the mini-golf course on a parcel of land acquired after a fire, turning the charred remains of a boarding house into his personal dream of summer vacation family fun. Her father had run the course as a young man, bringing his new wife to live in the apartment on the third floor, turning the ground floor into an ice-cream and soda counter. It had been her mother who suggested, after Grampa Buck passed away, that they convert his second floor dwelling to apartments: weekly rentals for summer vacationers, monthly rentals for UNH students in the off-season.

While Sofia watched, the beach filled in with

umbrellas and tents. Half a dozen kites flew over the boardwalk. Vacationing families were using the new bathhouse at the State Park—far better than the old one, she thought with a shudder. Kids and gulls shrieked from the high tide line, and the scent of Coppertone drifted over the piped-in music on the course. The kitten rested contentedly in the crook of her arm.

"You like it here, don't you?" She stroked one silky, steel gray ear. "You don't know that there's a whole world beyond this tacky town, a whole universe outside of New England."

The kitten's pleasant rumble was disturbed by the buzzing in her pocket. With her free hand, she fished out her phone. "Sofia Buck."

The tenants in 2B had clogged the toilet again. "I'll be right down."

Pocketing her phone, she shifted the small bundle on her arm. He blinked sleepily, stretching his skinny legs and flexing his fuzzy, half-dollar coin-sized paws.

"You're going to have to stay here alone for a few minutes. Can you do that?" Her companion yawned.

Sofia took him inside and carried him down the short hall, past the tiny bathroom and her parents' bedroom, to her childhood sanctuary. She focused on finding a pair of khaki shorts and a Buck's Landing polo, her glance coasting over the photos her father had set on the dresser sometime in the years between her departure and his death. There was a kind of madness in nostalgia, and Hampton Beach was not going to be her asylum.

Her guest began to knead the bedspread, and Sofia scooped him up. The kitten squeaked in protest. "No way, little man. This is the people bed, not the cat bed." She shut the bedroom door firmly behind her.

Plopping him down on the sofa, she headed for the utility closet. She grabbed a pair of long rubber gloves, a bucket, mop, and plunger. Giving the kitten a stern look, she said, "Be good."

She jogged down the stairs to the second of the two rental apartments that made up the second floor. This week, a family from upstate New York had 2B. During their brief exchange on Saturday afternoon, the mother had fretted over her.

"I'm so sorry to hear about your Dad, honey. He was such a nice man. Nick and I have been renting this place since before we got married. He was part of our vacation tradition."

Sofia had murmured the correct responses before showing them a few of the updates she'd arranged for over the past few weeks, including wireless internet. If she was going to be trapped in this place, she was at least going to be able to access the rest of the world from her laptop.

Pinning on her brightest smile, she knocked on the door. The mother opened the door. Her small child, a kindergartener named after a character from a movie—Trinity?—peered out from behind her legs.

"Hey, Sophie." The mother pushed a mop of sweaty curls from her forehead. "We're just heading across to the beach. Thanks for taking care of this."

Sofia swallowed the name correction that surfaced on her tongue. "Have fun. The waves are up this morning."

Thankfully, the toilet was only clogged with an abundance of quilted toilet paper. As she worked the plunger, she wondered what the fascination was with little kids and toilet paper rolls. Sofia cleaned up behind herself and locked the unit. She stowed the supplies back in her apartment, washed her hands, and poured herself a cup of coffee. Leaning on the counter to write up a to-do list, she ticked off her duties for the day.

The water in the fountain shared by the fourth and fifteenth holes was looking brackish, and she was running low on paper goods. Buck's Landing wasn't enough in the black to warrant a delivery service, which meant she'd be trucking over to Manchester for provisions and to stop at the pool supply place. And, at some point, she was going to have to call someone about the kitten.

She stood upright so quickly she nearly rapped her head on the upper cabinets. The kitten!

Her gaze flicked to the sofa, where a slight depression in her mother's once-favorite throw pillow was the only evidence of the feline adventurer's existence. She clicked her tongue and kissed the air in her apartment, willing the gray ball of fluff to appear from beneath some piece of furniture.

For twenty minutes she scoured her apartment for him, but the kitten was nowhere to be found. She was impressed. It was essentially a four room home. Her bedroom, the cramped-but-functional bathroom, her parents' bedroom, and the living space, with a single line of countertops and cabinets along one wall to hold the kitchen appliances. The dining table served as a visual separator for the room. When her efforts proved fruitless, she upped the ante. But a saucer of half-and-half and a bowl of chunk light tuna didn't coax the little monster out either. It wasn't until she went to the outside landing that she realized where he was.

The ghost of a smile played over her lips at the sight. Her furry friend had scaled another miniature landmark on the course. Not just any landmark, but the twelve-foot replica Easter Island head at the seventeenth hole.

Down again, out onto the course she went, grabbing the ladder from the utility room.

Amy spotted her coming. "He's awfully cute. Will you keep him?"

"I'm sure the little beast belongs to someone." Sofia propped the ladder against the statue and spoke to the three parties queued up at the tee. "Play through, folks. Amy will comp you all a soft-serve in the snack bar for your trouble." Amy herded everyone through while Sofia surveyed the head, looking for the best path to get to her little pal, who batted a passing white butterfly and mewed at her from his perch.

"Well, I know what I'm going to call you when I find you." Silas Wilde pushed up to standing, brushing a fine dusting of beach sand from his knees. He gave up hope that the little thing had only gone to ground under the sofa; he was fairly certain he was talking to an empty room. So far, the kitten his sister had given him at the beginning of the summer—a housewarming gift, or so Mallory claimed—had escaped his apartment no less than ten times, this last time managing, Silas feared, to get out of the building altogether.

He made a cursory examination of the bathroom and

efficiency kitchen before taking the back stairway down to the Atlantis Market, the convenience store and gift shop that was his new livelihood, half-hoping the kitten was playing with the mops and brooms in the hallway. When his search disappointed him, he headed into the Market. His older sister's oldest son, Theo, looked up from the register. He was ringing up a big sale: two beach chairs, a soft-sided cooler, and a picnic's worth of bottled water, soda, and junk food.

Silas had developed a great affection for impulse beachgoers.

"Cat got out again," he said.

Theo laughed. "I've got everything taken care of."

Silas let himself out through the store's front door, leaving Theo to handle the morning beachcombers in search of a snow globe of the Casino Ballroom, a new pair of flip-flops, or aloe gel. "Hopefully, I won't be gone more than a half hour. I've got my phone."

Silas had traced the New England coast north from New York City six months earlier, abandoning Interstate 95 in Boston to weave a northbound route along route 1 and 1A, in a Jeep Wrangler he'd bought from the Want Ads. A thousand times, his breath was stolen by the pewter sea and the rocky shoreline, peppered with stretches of coarse sand beaches and faded boardwalks, but something about Hampton Beach called to him. Following the tug, he'd checked into a motel a block inland, one of the few open in the frigid winter months, and fallen asleep to the north wind wailing over the snowy beach.

He'd thought Ocean Boulevard had stolen his heart in January, abandoned and near silent, save for some hardy year-round dwellers and a handful of businesses that defied the off-season. As he looked out over the summer expanse of state beach, pristine and already baking under a ninety-degree sun, the music of tourism and the magic of vacation coursed through him like the first swallow of a cold beer.

Had he still been in New York, sweltering in his Brooklyn walkup or hunched over his desk in the maze of cubicles on the litigation floor at Stern & Lowe, he might never have known the heady mix of kitsch and tradition that was Hampton. Owning a convenience store in a summer town was a good, long way from the document review sweatshop of corporate law.

Not even ten in the morning, and his worn R.E.M. tour tee-shirt was stuck to the small of his back. A bead of sweat rolled down his face, and he wiped it with the hem of the shirt. A gaggle of teenage girls wandered by in biki-nis, and one of them turned to give him a sassy grin, her eyes lingering over the flat expanse of his stomach. Silas watched them pass, doing his best not to appreciate the view too much.

He walked the perimeter of his building, examining a patch of newer cedar shingles, not yet weathered silver, while he looked for the cat. The previous owner had taken care of the Atlantis, even if his taste in interior decorating was a blend of seventies aesthetic and thrift store pragmatism. Silas called to the kitten with the whistle and click combination he'd found seemed to attract the small adventurer.

It wasn't long before he heard the meow from over the fence. The kitten was small, but he had lungs and feet worth watching. Following the cries, he arrived at the gate of Buck's Landing. His next door neighbor's building was taller, casting his apartment into welcome shade for most of the day. The owner, Jimmy Buck, had passed away about a month ago, leaving the whole property to his estranged daughter.

The jury was still out on the new Buck at the Landing, as far as Silas was concerned. She'd breezed into town in a slick BMW sedan, holed up in her late father's apartment, and kept mostly to herself. He'd only seen her once in the three weeks she'd been in residence; she'd been hauling a huge suitcase out of the trunk of that Beamer. She had refused his friendly offer of help, called down over the railing from the porch roof that served as his deck. He'd watched Jimmy's daughter drag that luggage up the two flights of narrow exterior stairs to the apartment with equal parts amusement and distaste.

Silas recognized the young woman working the register at Buck's. Amy had pounded pavement before the last frost looking for a summer job, even coming into the Atlantis Market to see if he was hiring. Turning her down had been tough, so he'd been glad to hear Jimmy had hired her on for the summer. Later in the spring when he'd run the numbers and knew he could afford a part-timer, he'd hired his nephew Theo at his sister's insistence. Mallory was a persistent woman.

"Amy." He smiled. She was reading one of those creased and worn steamy beach novels that passed from rental to rental. He imagined this one had been up and down the strip. Amy stashed the novel under the counter.

"Mr. Wilde. Can I help you?"

"I'm wondering if you've seen a kitten around the place this morning."

Amy lit up like the Funarama on a Saturday night. "Seventeenth hole. He's a troublemaker, huh?"

"You could say that. Thinking of calling him Houdini." He peered around the building towards the course. "Seventeen, you said?"

"Go on through, Mr. Wilde."

Silas couldn't help inspecting Jimmy Buck's Astroturf and the gravel paths that wound between the holes as he walked. Jimmy had been a good neighbor in the few months they'd known one another. The older man had introduced himself immediately following the first evening Silas spent in the apartment over the Atlantis; Jimmy had turned up on the welcome mat with a pair of to-go coffees and a half-dozen box of donuts. They'd grown close before his passing. Jimmy had told him stories about his family, mainly centered on his daughter's childhood, and had often confided in Silas that he wished he had more time and resources to put into the endless maintenance the property required.

There were changes at Buck's Landing, Silas noted. He had to admit, they were for the better. The paths were weeded, their gravel leveled. The turf and obstacles had been cleaned, and the greens patched in the worn spots. The music Jimmy had favored leaned toward classic country and western, so much so that Silas considered loaning the man his collection of Police and U2 CDs. Today he appreciated the thump of bass and electronic warble of Auto-Tune. The younger Buck knew what the kids listened to, anyway.

He heard Jimmy's daughter before she came into view. Unlike the overproduced pop-princess voice on the sound system, hers was a smoky voice that belonged in a speakeasy.

He rounded the corner at the sixteenth hole and burst out laughing. There was Houdini, surveying his kingdom from the top of the Easter Island head, his posture comically regal. The cat watched his would-be rescuer hoist herself from a short ladder by using the statue's left shoulder as a foothold.

"Come on, sweetheart," she cajoled, that bourbon voice pitched low. With an arm wrapped around the statue's head, she swung her leg over it, braced her other foot against its chest, and reached up for his cat.

Silas closed the distance between them and pushed his hair back with his sunglasses, the better to get an eye full of Jimmy Buck's mini-golf heiress. Silas took in the khaki shorts stretched across a toned rear and the strong, tanned legs, and briefly envied the statue, with his cement face pressed against that body.

"That's one lucky statue," he said with a chuckle. "I see you found my cat."

ARROGANT BASTARD. SOFIA'S CHEEKS WENT HOT AT THE thought of how she looked, clinging to the impassive face of the golf course obstacle. There was a click and whistle from the man, and the kitten flicked its ears. With a flash of gray fur and a scrabble of little nails, he streaked down from the monolith.

"I think his name is Houdini," the man laughed.

Sofia couldn't tell if he was laughing at his own joke, at the cat's name, or at her predicament.

She swung her leg towards the ladder. When she'd taken a leave from her position as the event planner for the DeVarona hotel in Washington, DC to return to Hampton Beach and sort out her father's property, she'd expected a hot, miserable summer of tourists in cheap tee-shirts spilling ice cream all over the run-down course. She hadn't been prepared for the changes to the old boulevard and the changes to Buck's Landing. She hadn't been prepared to get caught halfway up a Polynesian deity's face by her surfer-boy next door neighbor, but she was accustomed to damage control. She could face some local guy who'd lost his cat. When her foot missed and kicked the ladder instead of landing on a rung, she swore roundly and hung on to the cement.

To her horror, a pair of male hands steadied her, holding the backs of her thighs. The cheery conversations from the parties playing the course were gone, replaced by giggles and whispering.

"Easy now. I've got you." Her rescuer grasped her waist and lowered her to the turf. She sucked in a breath. It wouldn't do to fly off the handle in front of paying customers. Spinning around, she got a good look at her next door neighbor.

"You must be Jimmy's daughter," he said. The little gray cat sat on his broad shoulder like a pirate's parrot, delicately grooming one of his white-stockinged paws. "Thanks for helping out this little troublemaker. I'm Silas Wilde, your—"

"Next door neighbor, yes." She leveled him with her coolest managerial look and held out a hand. "Sofia Buck." His hands were big, she thought, watching hers disappear into his grip. And warm. His smile wrinkled his eyes, but she judged him to be near her age. From his shoulder, the kitten offered her his freshly groomed foot. His serious, whiskered expression charmed. "And you're Houdini."

Silas reached up and plucked the cat off his shoulder. "He's new, still getting the hang of being neighborly."

"I'd suggest locking your door, but he got out of my locked apartment earlier." She flicked an eyebrow at the pair. The gray kitten fit in his hand like a toy. "He's already been up the tree at hole twelve this morning."

Silas laughed, taking the measure of the so-called tree. Turning the kitten around to face him, he went nose-to-nose with his feline. "No more causing trouble for Ms. Buck. Though she does look fantastic stretched out on the moai."

Sofia snorted. "I am standing right here."

Silas turned his gaze on her. His eyes were the exact cool blue-gray of the Atlantic and his messy, honey-colored waves, pushed away from his face by a pair of sport sunglasses, were streaked summery blond. She felt his appraisal sweep over her. "So you are."

"Excuse me?" A barrel-chested man in a Red Sox tee-shirt was tapping his putter on the gravel. "Can we play?"

Sofia suppressed a grin as the sunburnt woman at his side smacked his upper arm and shushed him under her breath. "Please. I was just clearing up a hazard on the hole." She turned to Silas. "Mr. Wilde?"

"Silas." He stepped off the turf, Houdini settled in the crook of his arm. "And I've got to get back to the store."

Sofia flashed a smile at the golfers. "Enjoy your game."

She followed Silas's retreating form toward the gate, indulging in the fantastic view of his ass in hibiscus patterned surf shorts. When he stopped short, she very nearly crashed into him.

"Sofia," he said. "Let Houdini and I buy you a drink tonight."

She blinked. "No." Her manners surfaced. "Thank you, but no."

He scratched the cat's chin. "You've made the lady angry, you monster." His gaze was warm when he turned to her. "Another time, then."

Grab a blanket and a picnic and spend the summer on Hampton Beach, at Buck's Landing.

DAMSELFLY INN

AN EXCERPT

CHAPTER 1

*J*oss Fuller was daydreaming about his mother's tomato pie when lightning struck the Damselfly Inn.

He'd watched the storm smudge the horizon on the drive into town, marveled at the tumble of thunderheads sweeping across Lake Champlain towards Thornton, Vermont. By the time he crested the last rise, heading west towards his parents' farm on County Road, the rain was coming down hard.

Driving into the snaps of electricity in the sky and the deep growls of thunder over the valley of pasture and marsh where he'd grown up, Joss was considering a cold beer in front of some pre-season football. That, and the difference between one slice of roasted tomatoes, cheddar, basil, and his mother's ribbon-worthy cornmeal crust, or two.

The bolt that took out the huge maple tree in his parents' neighbor's side yard took Joss by surprise. His first thought was that the Swifts' place had been struck.

His second was to haul his pickup back into the road. Between the distraction and the gusting wind, he'd almost ditched the truck. When the limb that shaded the house's third floor snapped like a broken bone, leaving a steaming, ragged wound in the tree, Joss realized the lightning hadn't hit the actual building, but the damage was done. The limb had punched its way through the old Victorian's skin, puncturing the roof of what had once been a thoroughly neglected cluster of attic rooms, complete with clanking plumbing and shadowy gables.

The rain would likely prevent anything from burning, but there could very well have been guests in that attic room. He'd heard from his mom that the new owner–an innkeeper –had transformed the cobwebby attic into a bridal suite. Getting an invitation to see it was his mother's new project.

The innkeeper had become a favorite customer at the Fuller Dairy since her arrival in the valley earlier that summer. Joss wasn't sure if his mother was trying to fix him up or whether she just liked the newcomer, but Nan Grady had been a popular topic.

He'd noticed her around. You couldn't not notice someone new in a town like Thornton. With the college kids mostly gone for the summer, new faces stuck out, and hers was a pretty one.

He'd figured on making her acquaintance before too long. His best friend Jack and Jack's sister Kate were the reason she'd relocated to Thornton. It was only a matter of time before they were all in the same place at the same time.

He hadn't figured on the storm intervening.

Joss was already pulling into the Swifts' driveway–not

the Swifts' house, the Damselfly Inn, he reminded himself as he passed the understated carved sign–when the lights started snapping on inside the house, marking a trail from the apartment over the garage, down through the kitchen and into the front hall. He was pounding on the front door when the upstairs hall lit up, but the front door was locked, and the rest of the inn stayed dark.

NAN GRADY WAS TRACING GLOSSY LETTERING ACROSS A misdirected postcard when her house split open.

Greetings from Myrtle Beach S.C.! The card was a vintage-styled one, with each drop-shadowed block letter featuring a scene from the beach. She turned it over to read the note, to mull over the intended recipient. The handwriting was young – full and looping.

> *Danny, it's not this pretty where we live, but the beach is awesome. I miss you. Maybe you can come down here some time. It's warmer than Vermont anyway. Love, Ellie*

The postcard was addressed to Danny B. (heart, flower, star), 203 County Road, Thornton, VT. It had arrived that afternoon, nearly lost in the myriad catalogs, flyers, and bills in the mail. Something about the sender's bittersweet tone gave Nan pause. She carried it upstairs to her apartment, meaning to drop it in her purse for her next run into town. She suspected Gary at the Thornton Post Office would know exactly who Danny B. was.

Myrtle Beach sounded like a perfect alternative to the late summer collision of weather fronts currently heaving itself down from the Adirondacks. Outside, the early evening sky had gone gunmetal gray, roiling with clouds. The rain was static, punctuated by sharp cracks of thunder, and Nan could hear the wind buffeting the walls of the old house.

The storm continued its tantrum as it drove eastward, rushing up to and over the Green Mountains like water over a spillway. Rain pelted down, blown nearly horizontal, and the huge maple tree behind the inn groaned in protest.

There would be a mess to clean up in the yard in the morning.

She'd come upstairs to wait out the thunderstorm in the snug comfort of her apartment over the garage.

It was a disorienting feeling still, the newness of owning this grand old house, but living in two rooms that were only attached to it by the stairs off the kitchen, stairs whose walls framed the breezeway between the house and the garage. It was a heady feeling, though, owning the gracious yellow Victorian, opening it to travelers, hosting treasured memories, making a home for herself in this town she was quickly coming to love.

Nan turned the card over one last time, imagining thick South Carolina heat and the light tease of seabreeze. White heat lit up her living room, throwing everything into Hitchcock-esque relief for a heartbeat; when the thunder shattered the air no more than a half-second later, the lights blinked and the house shook with the impact.

She was on her feet and running for the stairs, pausing only to grab her Maglite from the coffee table drawer, and the card fluttered, forgotten, to rest on the braided rug.

A cold wind tumbled down from the third floor to meet her in the foyer.

With a hard knot of dread already forming in her stomach, she raced up to the third floor landing. She yanked open the door to the Adirondack Suite with her heart pounding.

The scene inside the room struck her like a fist. Rain was pouring in through the remains of the gabled roof, lumber and insulation hanging down like broken bones and torn flesh. The hot smell of ozone was fresh in the air. Shingles and debris littered the floor. The silk drapes whipped and snapped at the sills. A limb from the ancient maple tree that grew next to the house lay across the sleigh bed, its raw end sizzling.

"Oh, god. No," she said aloud to the empty room, her voice swallowed by the noise of the storm. "No."

She forced herself to loosen the death grip in which she held the doorknob. She forced herself to inhale and exhale. If she let herself cry, she would fall apart entirely.

The rain water was pooling in the dips and hollows of the old pine floorboards. She cast around for something to soak up the puddles, for something to catch the deluge. *A paper cup,* she thought with a hysteric giggle, like that song from the Eighties. Shock was making her head fuzzy. She had a bucket and towels in the hall utility closet, but what the hell was she going to do about the hole in her roof?

Out in the hallway, she paused. Someone was banging on the front door; a voice muffled by the storm and three floors of space was calling. She waited, counting the thumping of her heart – one-two, one-two, one-two – but the pounding was persistent.

She jumped when a man's voice called her name from downstairs.

"Miss Grady? Hello! Is anyone up there? Hello?"

She thought of her phone, waiting for her back in her apartment. The man calling knew her name, but she had no idea who she was facing, alone in the dark house in a storm. She gripped the flashlight tightly and started slowly down the stairs.

They all reached the second story landing at the same time. Nan stopped short in relief. Walt Fuller, the dairy farmer from down the road, stood in the second floor hallway in a dripping slicker and muddy boots, with a younger man in a sweatshirt and ball cap at his side.

"Miss Grady? Are you all right?" Walt asked, catching his breath.

Nan almost laughed at the absurdity of the question. Not by a long shot. There was a tree branch in her bridal suite. There were muddy boot tracks on the hallway runner. Panic welled up in her chest again, but she forced it down when she saw Walt's expression. He must have heard the lightning strike, seen her roof, and come running to find out if she'd been underneath it.

She was all right. The third floor was another story.

"I'm fine, Mr. Fuller. The room upstairs –" She started to shake and pressed her hand against her mouth, fearing she might cry after all.

"Come on down to the kitchen, now, Miss Grady. Molly will make tea for you, and Joss here's going to go take a look at your damage." Walt gestured to his companion.

As Walt Fuller put a hand on her shoulder and steered her towards the stairs, she looked back at the younger man. His eyes were the same shade as the thunderheads outside, and he exuded quiet competence in a way that momentarily quelled the panic brewing in her belly.

"I'll be down in a bit." He spoke to his father, but his eyes stayed on her.

In the kitchen, Molly Fuller was boiling water and getting out the tea and teapot.

"I went ahead and poked around your kitchen, hon. I hope that's ok," she said to Nan, before turning to her eyes to her husband. "How bad is it?"

"Joss'll tell us in a minute. I sent him on up." Walt joined his wife at the counter.

Nan was out of sorts watching her neighbor commandeer her kitchen. "Mr. and Mrs. Fuller, thank you –"

"None of that, now," Molly interrupted. "We've barged into your house; we're past formalities. I'm Molly, he's Walt, and we're all neighbors. We take care of our own. Now, I put a fair amount of sugar in this one. It'll help with the shock."

The mug was solid and warm; the tea sweet and strong. She felt the panic begin to dissipate, the knot of dread loosen. She took a deep breath, then remembered her manners.

"I hope you'll call me Nan, then." She watched Walt take his place next to his wife; he fit there like a missing piece. "There are cookies from Sweet Pease on a plate under that pie dome, if you'd like."

Molly smiled. "Your mother raised you well."

"My gran, actually." Words tumbled out, as much to fill the air as to provide them with her history. "My grandparents raised me. My mother passed away when I was small, and my father was never what you'd call present."

She flushed, feeling she'd revealed too much. "Joss... is your son?" she asked, hoping to shift the topic of conversation away from her rootless past.

"He is," answered Molly. "Short for Josiah. Contractor and carpenter, so you're in good hands. He'll get things buttoned up for you tonight, and I'm sure he'll come back in the morning to do a proper estimate, if you'd like." Molly spoke with a certainty that brooked no refusal.

The man himself walked into the kitchen, wiping a hand on his jeans; he carried his wet sweatshirt and hat in the other. Rain clung to his hair, leaving damp streaks on his Thornton Hornets tee as it beaded and rolled off.

"Mom, my ears are burning." There was a smile in his voice.

Something like envy kindled in her heart. The Fullers had that intangible ease that came with closeness and familiarity. They were family.

Molly introduced them, "Josiah, this is Nan Grady. Nan, our son, Josiah Fuller."

"A pleasure, Nan, circumstances notwithstanding." He reached for her hand. "And please," he said with a wry look at his mother, "Call me Joss."

"Joss." She put her hand in his. Their eyes met over the handshake, and a current flared between them. His hands were calloused, warm, pleasantly rough. She wondered how they would feel sliding up her back, running through her hair.

She was sure she must be blushing.

"Well, son, what needs to be done tonight?" Walt asked, interrupting her wayward thoughts. She almost laughed; she was more in shock than she'd realized.

Nan pulled her hand away, but she wasn't sure what to

do with it. It took her a moment to realize that Joss was speaking to her.

"Have you got tarps and rope? Tie-downs? I'm going to get up on the roof and cover the hole up until morning. The rain's clearing off, but I don't want to leave that hole exposed. You're lucky," he said. "There's nothing vital in that section of ceiling and the structure's not too badly compromised."

Maybe she'd imagined the heat, the spark between them. Joss didn't seem affected by it at all. Gran had always called her an old soul. She supposed it must be true. At thirty-one, her most devoted relationship was with a century-old house, and the first good looking man she'd taken a moment to notice in six months had set her skin humming.

"I've got some tie-downs in my car, but no tarps." She wished she'd thought to buy them on one of her many trips up to South Burlington for supplies.

"That's no trouble at all." He shrugged and turned to Walt. "Pop, I'll need to borrow some from you, and come back."

"I'll help you get some from the barn," Walt said. "Let's not keep the poor girl up all night."

"I think I'll be up anyway." Nan sighed.

"Nonsense, Nan," Molly said. "I'll stay to help you clean up."

Flustered by her neighbors' generosity, Nan started to tidy the tea tin and sugar bowl. "Please, Molly, Walt." She was embarrassed but resolute. "I can handle it tonight."

Molly's gaze met hers before she got up and cleared the mugs. Nan hoped Molly understood. She needed to fall apart and pull herself back together again in peace.

Molly rinsed out the teapot and dried her hands. She took a key from her pocket and set it on the island. "You're going to want to put that key back under the mat."

Nan stared at the key as Molly bustled out the kitchen door, followed by her men. In all the panic and confusion, she hadn't given a thought to how the Fullers had gotten into the house. She was grateful Molly Fuller had figured out where her spare key was; she supposed beneath the doormat wasn't a very original hiding place.

"Molly, wait!" she called. "Take the key. If I ever need it, I'll know where to look."

Joss, who was the last to go through the kitchen door, turned and took the key from her outstretched hand.

～

Check into the Damselfly Inn, and fall in love with Thornton Vermont.